BACHELOR'S END

BACHELOR'S END

•

Carol Reddick

AVALON BOOKS
NEW YORK

PRINTED IN THE UNITED STATES OF AMERICA
ON ACID-FREE PAPER
BY HADDON CRAFTSMEN, BLOOMSBURG, PENNSYLVANIA

To my own childhood sweetheart,
Randy,
and to Devon, Kelsey, and Rebecca.

To Mom and Dad
for listening all those years.

Special thanks to Sandie Bricker—
mentor, friend, cheerleader,
and
sister-in-faith.

Prologue

"**W**ait up, you guys!"

Gillian ran as fast as her skinny, twelve-year-old legs would go, but her smooth-bottomed Keds kept slipping on the slick cow manure, making it impossible to keep up with the older boys ahead.

"No way, Sparky. Go back home!" Seth Connor didn't bother to slow down or turn around as he and his friend tried to outrun the girl behind them.

Gillian slipped again as she watched Seth and chunky Charlie Mahoney disappear around a bend up ahead. This time her feet flew out from underneath her and she landed on her stomach with a thud, knocking the breath from her lungs and her glasses off her face. She lay, dazed and prone, in the grass-encrusted cow dung for a moment, certain her paralyzed lungs would never draw another breath. Tears of frustration prickled at the back of her eyes, but she refused to give in to the need to cry, especially with Mr. Mackey's stupid cows witnessing her humiliation with their big, brown moon-pie eyes.

She picked herself up out of the slimy cow mush, retrieved her glasses, and renewed her determination not to

1

be left behind again. *Not this time, Seth Connor,* she thought.

Drawing deep, calming breaths into her aching lungs, she slowed her ragged breathing and racing heart. *Listen, Gillian, listen,* she chided herself. *Do what Daddy told you when he took you squirrel hunting.* Pushing her sweaty tangle of hair behind her ear, she listened keenly as the boys thrashed through the tall grass between the pasture and the woods. They were much further ahead of her now, moving toward the river, and they obviously weren't trying to be quiet. But it wouldn't have mattered if they'd been quiet as church mice since, looking ahead, she could see that the waist-high grass was flattened where they'd trampled through, giving their direction away.

Quietly, carefully, Gillian followed their trail until it ended abruptly at the base of a gnarled old oak on the bank of the Little Tennessee. Scattered footprints were evident in the soft brown mud between the river and the oak. She scanned the river for movement in case the boys had gone in for a swim, but, seeing nothing other than the gentle flow of the current over river rock, she laughed triumphantly and raised her eyes to search for the boys in the branches above.

"Ha!" she shouted to the Converse sneakers balanced on a gnarled limb directly above her head. "I found you, Seth Connor, so you can just come on down here right now."

Silence was the only reply.

"I know you're up there, and I'll just wait down here until you come down. You can't stay up there forever, you know."

There was still no answer.

Switching tactics, she circled the base of the oak, looking for a foothold. Finding no obvious way up, she stamped her foot in frustration and reverted to demanding. "I mean it! Come down here right now, or I'm gonna tell your daddy that you were making out in the dugout with your hands up Mary Jo Martin's shirt last Friday night."

That did the trick.

"Whew hew! Way to go, Seth," Charlie called from his perch nearby.

"Go on, Gillian. Go back home," Seth replied, calling her bluff. "You aren't going to tell my daddy anything, and you know it."

"I will too!" she shouted up at him. "You promised you'd go fishing with me."

"We're not going fishing right now, stupid," Charlie hollered down. "We're going swimming."

"I'm not talking to you, Chunky." Gillian folded her arms across her stomach, more than prepared to wait them out. After all, they couldn't stay up in that tree forever. "And I'm not leaving, either."

Finally, two heads appeared from behind the main trunk, and she couldn't quite hide her smug smile, but her victory was short-lived. She barely had enough time to flinch and shriek before a falling river rock smacked her square between the eyes, knocking her glasses off her face and into the mud at her feet.

Charlie Mahoney's laughter added insult to injury. "Way to go, Seth. Good aim!"

Gillian was mortified, in pain, and horrifyingly close to crying, which she *never* did. For a moment, she was frozen, unable to make herself move. Then suddenly she was racing back through the tall grass and mushy manure, past the forest and Mr. Mackey's stupid cows. Her head was throbbing, and she could feel a trickle of sweat or blood—she wasn't sure which—running down her face, but she refused to slow down. Though her aching legs and lungs screamed for her to rest, she didn't stop running until she reached the safety of home and the comforting embrace of her father's arms. Too late, she remembered her fallen glasses, but nothing could make her go back to retrieve them. She'd never, *ever* talk to Seth Connor again.

Then, as her father cradled her face in his strong, capable hands and examined her wound, Gillian did what she'd sworn she'd never do, even when she'd caught Seth kissing that ugly Mary Jo Martin. She cried her aching twelve-year-old heart out over a boy.

That was the last she saw of Seth Connor and chunky Charlie Mahoney. A few days, a new pair of glasses, and eight stitches later, she and her mother left Ruby Valley, North Carolina, Seth Connor, and her father behind—one of them vowing never to remember, the other vowing never to forget.

Chapter One

Gillian Guy stretched her arms over her head and rolled over to bury her face in her fluffy feather pillow, hiding her eyes from the early light of day. Moaning softly, she tried to keep the morning at bay, but it wasn't to be denied. She groaned and dragged open her sleepy eyes, pushing her wild tangle of hair away from her face, then swung her legs over the side of the bed and perched on the edge.

Three days of cleaning glassware and moving furniture around her ancient antique shop had taken its toll on her body. Her arms were tired, her shoulders and back sore with fatigue. She rolled her shoulders around to relieve some of the tightness and winced. She considered herself physically fit, power walking or running four or five days a week, but today she felt more like seventy-seven than the twenty-seven she was.

She contemplated crawling back beneath the covers with one last longing glance at the rumpled sheets, but knew she had to get up and moving. There was still so much more to be done. Dusting, cleaning, moving . . . and that was just the beginning. It would probably take an army to accomplish the task, rather than just herself and one lone handyman.

Her handyman! She'd forgotten all about him. A glance
at the clock confirmed that she'd overslept. He was due at
eight and it was nearly that now. With a cry of dismay, she
jumped out of bed, raced down the tiny hallway to the
bathroom, and skidded to a halt at the porcelain sink. She
was just turning on the water to brush her teeth when she
heard the knock at the door.

"Oh, blast it," she muttered, then hastily shoved the
toothbrush around inside her mouth, rinsed, spit, and raced
to open the door.

"I'm sorry to keep you waiting . . ." she began, only to
lose track of what she'd been about to say. Whatever she'd
expected a handyman to look like, it wasn't this gorgeous
guy gracing her doorstep.

"I haven't been out here long," he said, extending his
hand.

Gillian held out her own hand to shake, but he reached
beyond it to her face, where he gently rubbed a thumb at
one corner of her mouth. Momentary surprise rooted her to
the spot before she jumped back to put safe distance between them. "Hey!" she exclaimed, ready to use some self-
defense moves if necessary.

"Toothpaste," he explained, dark eyes twinkling.

Embarrassment stained her cheeks. *So much for first im-
pressions.* In an effort to regain the upper hand, she extended hers once again. "I'm Gillian Guy, the new owner
of Bachelor's End Antiques."

He took her hand and held it in his warm grasp, tightening his grip momentarily before setting it free. "Welcome
home, Gillian. You don't remember me, do you?"

She let her gaze roam over his face. There was something about him, something familiar in his dark eyes, his
voice. And then he smiled. A lovely, lopsided grin that
jangled her memory.

"Seth?" She could see it was so when his devil-may-care

smile deepened, causing his left cheek to dimple in a very familiar way.

Suddenly, she was twelve again, staring up at Seth as he dropped the rock on her, and all the hurt she'd felt came rushing back to the surface. "Go away," she said, giving the door a good, hard shove. It was childish, she knew, but there it was. She was still mad at him for heaving a rock on her head, and couldn't think of one good reason to renew their acquaintance.

His hand caught the door and held it firmly, preventing her from shutting it in his face. "Hey, hang on a minute, Sparky. You asked me to come, remember?"

"Don't call me that! I hated it then, and I hate it now." She came very near to childishly stomping her foot, but stopped herself just in time. "Just go. I'm too busy for this. In fact, I have someone coming over any minute, so I'd appreciate it if you'd leave."

Seth laughed and moved inside, shutting the door firmly behind him, forcing Gillian to retreat a few steps or go nose to nose with him. She didn't like to back down from a confrontation, but she did like to choose her battles wisely. Since Seth had seven or so inches on her and at least seventy-five pounds, putting distance between them seemed the prudent thing to do.

They stood like that, sizing each other up, for what felt an eternity to Gillian. His eyes swept her from head to toe and back again, measuring her mettle, she was sure, while she simply crossed her arms, arched a brow, and tried to wither him with the look of haughty disdain she usually reserved for swindler antique dealers. She'd walked away with treasures won on her own terms more often than not, just as she planned on handling Seth's intrusion on her own terms now. Any minute, he'd realize he was messing with fire. He'd know without a shadow of a doubt that she wasn't that desperate little girl who'd chased him all over the valley that summer so long ago. She was an intelligent, savvy, self-assured woman of the new millennium, and he'd be wise not to cross her.

"You're expecting company in that?" His eyes dropped from hers, traveling slowly down her body and up again.

Gillian looked down, horrified to see she was still wearing her nightclothes, a clingy pink silk camisole with matching boxers. Refusing to let him know she was embarrassed to the roots of her hair, she quickly put on an attitude of nonchalance, brandishing it like a sword in the thick of battle. "Yes, I am. I've only been back in town a few days, but I don't believe in wasting any time. He's due here any minute, so if you'll just be on your way . . ."

Seth flashed a devilish grin and, before Gillian could even guess what he was doing, scooped her up in his arms and nestled her firmly against his solid chest. "Then, let's get started, sweetheart," he teased, obviously enjoying this new tactic of hers. "I wouldn't want to keep you waiting."

Gillian gave up all pretense of disinterest and began to struggle as he moved toward the hallway that led to her bedroom. What was he thinking? He may have been her friend once upon a time, but that had been a very, very long time ago, for heaven's sake. "Don't you dare, Seth Connor. Put me down this instant! What do you think you're doing, you big bully!"

That brought him to a halt, though it didn't gain her release. She knew her eyes were shooting sparks, but it wasn't having the desired effect on him. In fact, his eyes were filled with laughter. "Whether you realize it not, I *am* the man you've been waiting for."

Hot color flooded her cheeks again as she childishly struggled even harder, knowing he was teasing her, yet unable to remain still in his arms. She opened her mouth to blast him, but stopped when she saw the look in his eyes.

The teasing light was gone, suddenly replaced by something much more intense. Helplessly, she ceased struggling as he slowly slid her to her feet and, with a feather-light touch, traced the tiny scar on her forehead.

"I did that, didn't I?" he asked.

Gillian swallowed and tried to find her voice. Her fingers traced where his had touched just a moment before. The scar. It had faded over the years and was hardly discernable, but he'd seen it. She sighed. "It's ancient history."

Seth shook his head, reached his hand out toward her, then dropped it back by his side, as though knowing his touch could bring no comfort. "It needs to be aired out, Gillian, or it'll always stand between us. It was just an accident, you know."

Gillian blinked back the tears that suddenly filled her eyes, hating herself for her emotional weakness. This was so childish. It had all happened so long ago. She wasn't that straggly little ragamuffin she'd once been, so why did it still hurt to remember?

"There is no us, Seth, and there's no need to apologize. That was a long time ago, and I'm all grown up now. An entirely different person." She turned her back to him and walked to the front door, gathering her composure about her like a blanket to ward off a winter chill. Once, she'd been a hot-tempered tomboy, but she'd worked hard to mold herself into the image of a composed businesswoman. She'd managed her mother's antique business single-handedly, and ruthlessly faced down the toughest competitors at auction houses across the South. It would take more than an unexpected reunion with Seth Connor to break her and make her expose her vulnerability. With what she hoped would pass for indifference, she gestured toward the door she now held open. "Please leave. I really am expecting somebody, and I need to get dressed."

Seth didn't budge. In fact, he merely crossed his arms and raised one eyebrow in defiance of her order. "You were expecting *me*." He extended his hand and formally introduced himself. "Seth Connor of Valley Hardware. Co-owner, handyman, and jack-of-all-trades."

"You're kidding," she said, horrified by the unladylike snort of disbelief which escaped her nose.

Seth's smile assured her he wasn't. "I took over after Dad passed away and Uncle Bob reached retirement. My cousins, Elizabeth and Jackson, and I run it together now. She keeps the books, he manages the place, and I get stuck with the grunt work."

Well, that figured. She'd brought this on herself; she really should have known better. The Connors had owned the hardware store forever.

"I see. Well, make yourself at home then," she said, gesturing toward the well-worn couch in her tiny living room. "I'll just run and change into something more appropriate, and then I'll walk you over to the shop."

"Don't change on my account," he said with a wink. "Pink's my favorite color."

Gillian's cheeks bloomed as she scurried away to the safety of her bedroom, shutting the door firmly on Seth's laughter and locking it tightly for good measure.

Seth restlessly prowled the tiny living room looking for something that might give him some insight into this grown-up version of Gillian, but there was nothing. It looked like old Edward Keeney had sold her the place lock, stock, and barrel. Dust and cobwebs too, he noted, trailing a finger across an end table, then wiping it clean on his old work jeans. The room offered no clues, but it did raise some questions. *What kind of woman would buy a dump like this?* he wondered. *And why?*

He wasn't sure what he'd expected when she'd opened the door, but it sure hadn't been a drop-dead gorgeous woman with that wild mane of auburn hair. He tried to reconcile his memory of a gangly twelve-year-old waif with the full-grown armful of woman he'd just had the pleasure of holding. It just wouldn't compute.

She'd been such a scruffy thing as a kid, sort of like a stray pup, always tagging along with him and his friends, making a pest out of herself. To be perfectly honest, he hadn't really minded. He knew he'd been the closest thing to a best friend she'd ever had in the valley. But that had been a very long time ago. Now she was nothing more than a beautiful stranger and potential client.

He checked his watch, wondering how much longer she'd be, then realized she'd only been gone a few minutes. He dropped down to the couch, then sprang right back up again feeling unusually restless.

When he'd paced the living room one too many times he worked his way to the tiny kitchen to wait for her return. It was obvious she hadn't been here long. It looked like everything was still in boxes except the coffeemaker. The place looked about like he'd figured it would since the Keeney brothers hadn't been known for taking care of mundane little things like maintenance. He looked at the bare windows and what was visible of the old linoleum floor and started working lists and figures in his head. Wood for the windowsill and trim, curtain rod, paint for the walls and ceiling, labor to rip up the old flooring, maybe some ceramic tile to replace it. If she was on a budget, he could swing her a deal on something less expensive like vinyl flooring. Heck, if she just batted her lashes at him a time or two, he might do the labor for free.

Grinning like a fool, he pulled a chair away from the kitchen table and straddled it, recalling the look on her face when he'd called her Sparky. She'd hated that name when he gave it to her as a kid, and he'd been pretty sure it would rile her up today. He didn't usually try to provoke beautiful women, but he'd been irritated that she hadn't recognized him.

"If you have a minute, I'll put on some coffee," she said

as she entered the kitchen. Then, not waiting for a reply, she set about gathering the necessary items while he watched.

He was both relieved and disappointed to see she'd tamed that wild mass of hair into a ponytail and was dressed in cutoffs and a baggy old T-shirt. Her face was devoid of makeup, and all the more stunning for it. Her beauty was natural, her features classic.

"Have you had breakfast?" She turned, nearly catching him staring. He quickly averted his eyes as he shook his head. "I have bagels and cream cheese, but I haven't managed to locate the toaster yet so you'll have to have it untoasted." She took a couple of cups down from the cabinet, then rummaged through some boxes and produced napkins and sugar. "I hope you don't take cream. I haven't had time to shop yet. My priority is getting my business up and running as soon as possible. In a month, to be precise."

"A month?" He thought of the big, old house filled to the rafters with nothing better than garage-sale junk and frowned. He hated to disillusion her, but there was no way she could have the place open for business in a month. First of all, some of the things she'd most likely need to have done would probably require permits and Ruby Valley was notoriously slow at issuing those, though Seth had had some success at moving the process along more quickly now and again. "That's not much time."

"Time's a commodity I'm afraid I don't have. If I'm going to last through the winter, I've got to get it up and running in the black before the end of tourist season. What's that, the end of October?" She poured coffee into the cups she'd placed on the table, then set out a plate of bagels and sat down in the chair opposite him. "Failure is not an option."

So she was staying. Ruby Valley was to be her permanent home, not just a seasonal place of business. One question down, about ninety-nine more to go. "Do you have any idea how much work needs to be done on this place?" It was a rhetorical question, really, and he didn't expect an answer, but she surprised him.

"Actually, the place is a dump and needs a complete overhaul, but I have some ideas that'll let me get the place up and running while repairs are being done. That way, I'll be generating income to pay for the repairs, and maybe every once in a while I'll be able to afford some food too." She flashed a grin, but he could see a bit of fear in her eyes.

He watched as she sipped her coffee and then sliced a bagel, handing one half to him on a napkin and keeping one for herself. Concern had his thoughts churning. Did she really think that old junk shop was going to turn any kind of profit before winter? Antique shops, card and collectible shops, clothing shops, and ice cream parlors opened in a blaze of glory each summer and burned out just as quickly once the tourists were gone. If she didn't have enough money to survive in the red during her first year or two, her business would never make it and she'd be gone before she ever really started. Tourists were the key to success, and they'd take flight southward just as soon as the last leaf fell from the autumn trees.

"Seth?" Gillian's expression was puzzled, and he realized he'd missed something she'd said.

"I'm sorry," he said uneasily, wondering how deeply what he had to say was going to hurt her. He watched her eyes carefully as he continued. "I was thinking about what you said about needing to turn a profit by winter. That's not going to be as easy as you think, I'm afraid, especially way out here on the highway. The Keeneys had a hard go of it the past couple of years. I think that's why Edward was so eager to sell when his brother passed on."

Just as he suspected, her eyes took on a stubborn edge and her chin angled just a bit, so he carefully weighed his words, wanting to caution, rather than anger, her. "Do you have any experience at this sort of thing?"

He'd blown it. He knew by the way she so carefully set her cup back on the table without a sound and folded her arms across her chest that he'd phrased his question all wrong. "What I mean is . . ."

"I know what you meant." Each word was clipped, defensive. "You're worried that a little lady like me can't possibly know how to run a business on her own. Well, I don't have cousins to help me out here, Seth. I only have myself. My mother and stepfather aren't going to run up here from Florida and bail me out when things get tough, but I won't need for them to. I *do* have experience running an antique store, for your information, and I did it well. Bachelor's End will be a success because I'll make sure it is, and that's all there is to it, so you can rest your fears."

She scraped her chair back from the table and stood, hovering imperiously over him. She was all business. "If you're finished, I'll take you up to the shop." Then, she turned and walked out the kitchen door, not waiting to see if he followed along behind.

Well, so much for being concerned about her. It's not like he needed one more person to worry about, anyway. At last count he had his cousins and his crazy aunt all depending on him in one way or another, not to mention half the folks in the valley who figured he had forty-eight hours in his day compared to their own twenty-four. That's why he was counting the days until he could make his getaway to Charlotte and leave Ruby Valley far, far behind.

He pushed back from the table and took his cup to the sink, then followed her out the door and across the lawn to the big house which served as the antique shop, keeping a safe distance between them, giving her temper time to settle. It gave him more time to consider her. She'd been a spitfire as a kid, and though she'd grown into a woman, it was nice to see there was something of the old "Sparky" left.

"The Keeney brothers let things go," she said, as he joined her on the back porch and wiped his feet on the newspaper she was using as a doormat. "I think it's structurally sound; that's what the inspector's report says, anyway. But there are water stains on the ceiling in the parlor, probably from leaky plumbing, and I'm afraid the stair railing is going to tumble down, it's so rickety."

He watched and listened as she took him through the house, occasionally jotting down notes on the pad he kept in his back pocket. By the time they'd come full circle and were back downstairs in the shop's kitchen, he'd decided that he liked what he saw. The job wouldn't be as difficult or time consuming as he'd originally thought, and once the water-damaged ceiling was taken care of, she'd be able to use the entire downstairs area while he worked on the stair railing and the upstairs rooms. Maybe a month wasn't impossible after all.

"I'd wanted to get a second opinion before making a commitment, but time is of the essence and no one else is available right now. Do you think you can handle the job?"

He thought of the jobs that were piling up and the ten-hour days he'd been putting in and inwardly groaned. If he were a smart man, he'd tell her the truth and give her a start date of July, but he knew how badly she needed to get the place opened.

"Next week," he heard himself say, giving himself a mental kick for being such an idiot over a beautiful woman. "I'll just shuffle some jobs around and work a few extra hours to fit you in. In the meantime, I've got a friend who does plumbing. I'll send him over to fix those leaky pipes."

She beamed at him and extended her hand to seal the deal, nearly quivering with excitement. For a moment, he saw straight past the businesswoman to the child she'd once been and he felt an odd sense of recognition, like a homecoming. He suddenly realized he was still holding her hand, quickly released it, and took his leave.

As he pulled his pickup out onto the highway and headed toward town, he found himself grinning like a fool for the second time that morning.

Chapter Two

Seth eased his Ford pickup into his spot in front of Valley Hardware. Between his consult with Gillian, his scheduled jobs, and the emergency call-ins Elizabeth had beeped to him, he'd put in another ten-hour day. Exhaustion pulled at his brain, but he planned on staying awake long enough to grab some take-out and toss back a beer once he made it home. Then, he'd collapse into his recliner and sleep until bedtime. Tomorrow he'd get up at six and start all over again. Sunday would be his only day of rest, and that would be spent doing odd jobs around his own cabin and getting his laundry done.

Man, he needed a break. September couldn't come soon enough as far as he was concerned. His cousins Lizzie and Jackson would be on their own then, and he'd be in an air-conditioned office in Charlotte farming the grunt work out to employees. His employees. Well, his and Charlie's. That had a nice ring to it.

The shrill bleat of his beeper jarred him from his thoughts. Snatching it up to silence the irritating noise, he slammed out of his truck and strode into the store.

"Elizabeth, it's past six. I'm off the clock," he growled

as soon as he stomped into the office. "Whatever it is, it'll have to wait until tomorrow."

"Relax, tough guy." The petite Elizabeth didn't bat an eyelash at Seth's bluster.

"Yeah, you can say relax when you're sitting pretty in the a.c. all day." Taking the day's receipts and checks out of his pocket, he slapped them on the desk in front of her. "Here's some more work for you. See that you get it done before you leave for the night."

Coal black eyebrows wiggling wickedly, Lizzie shook her head. "No way, Cousin, I've got a date, and I won't be late."

Seth wasn't at all surprised since she had a date lined up more nights than not. Then again, so had he once upon a time when he'd wanted, but that was beside the point. "Suit yourself, Liz. Save it till later if you want. It's all going to be your headache soon anyway."

"So, then, why are you working your butt off, Seth?" she challenged. "You ever actually going to make that move you've been spouting off about? Charlie's been there for months and seems to be doing just fine without you."

"You can make all the cracks you want until September and then I'm gone. In the meantime, I'm working my butt off to make sure you don't sink the minute I walk out that door, smarty-pants."

Elizabeth laughed good-naturedly. "Always a smart-aleck reply and name calling . . . Oh! That reminds me why I paged you."

"To call me names?"

"No," she said thoughtfully, "though it does have its merits. I've got to head out soon, but I wanted to find out all the dirty details."

Seth pretended ignorance, though he knew exactly what she was talking about. "About what?"

"Don't go down that lane with me, Seth. You know what."

This game was a familiar one for the two of them: Lizzie pumping him for information, usually about his latest fling, Seth tossing out tidbits here and there to keep her satisfied. But today, Seth felt as though Lizzie was prying. He wanted to stop the gossip about Gillian, if possible, and if he gave even the tiniest tidbit to Lizzie, she'd have it spread clear to Bryson City by nightfall. No one ran with gossip faster, or more accurately, than his cousin, and there'd be plenty of folks in the valley who'd be happy to rekindle the dead embers of the past.

He wondered if Gillian realized that her return was sure to stir up old rumors. There'd been a lot of speculation about her mother's hasty departure and divorce followed by her father's remarriage so soon afterwards, and it was bound to resurface now that she'd returned. He didn't want to see her get hurt by things she'd had no control over.

"Come on, Seth. What's she like?" Liz prodded.

This time, he ignored her. "Where's Jackson?"

Annoyance flashed in her eyes. "What do I have to do? Go out there and check her out myself?"

"Yep."

"Oh, come on. Just tell me what she looks like. Is she fat? Wrinkled? Pregnant? Married?"

Married? He hadn't asked. He'd just assumed she was single. She'd mentioned her mother and stepfather, not a husband, but that didn't mean she didn't have one around somewhere, waiting to move up later when the house sold or something.

"I can't believe it." Liz pointed a perfectly manicured, lethal-looking nail at him. "She's been back in town for less than two weeks and you're already looking out for her. What do you think I'm going to do, pull her braids like I did when we were kids?"

Seth chuckled at the memory of the one and only time she'd tried. "Yeah, you tried, but Gillian gave you a bloody nose and you ran off crying." He laughed when Liz stuck her tongue out at him.

"Yeah, but you were there to rescue her if she'd needed it. I think you had a little crush on our Gillian," she teased. "Are you feeling a little residual puppy love? Is that why you're being so secretive?"

That was ridiculous, and he told her so. "I'm just trying to give her some time to settle in before the gossipmongers get started."

Liz sat back with a speculative look. "You *are* protecting her. Do you really think that's up to you? She's all grown up now, Seth. I'm sure she can look after herself."

He had to give her that much. "You may be right, Liz, but I sure don't have to be the one to start the rumors, and we both know if I tell you anything, that's just what'll happen."

The office door opened, interrupting their standoff, and Jackson Connor, Elizabeth's brother, popped his head inside. "Hey, Seth. I'm glad you're back. I could use a hand out here unloading the truck. Billy took off early to pick up his tux for the senior prom, so I'm on my own."

Relieved to have a reprieve from the inquisition, Seth left the office to help Jackson, leaving a very curious Elizabeth behind. If he knew his cousin, she'd be all over Gillian faster than ants on food at a picnic.

He pictured Gillian as she'd looked when she'd opened the door to him. Her hair had been wild about her face with strands streaming down to fall on her shoulders. Her eyes had been soft and sleepy, tinged with embarrassment at being caught unprepared and unprofessional. Then, just moments later, they'd flashed as frigid as an artic blast when he'd teased her. With a laugh, he had to concede to his cousin; Gillian was all grown up now, and he'd bet she could still hold her own against Elizabeth any day.

"What's so funny?" Jackson asked, joining Seth on his way through the storeroom.

"I was just laying odds on a cat fight."

Jackson playfully socked Seth in the arm as they walked out onto the loading dock behind the store. "Fighting over you again, are they? Enjoy it while it lasts. Once you move to Charlotte you'll be too busy with business to play around with the ladies' hearts. Liz and I heard Charlie hasn't had a date in nearly a year. I had to threaten to fire her to keep her from driving over there to save him. Sheesh. Women!"

Seth pulled on a pair of work gloves and grabbed a bag of fertilizer off the truck that was waiting at the loading dock. "I don't have time to play with them now, in case you haven't noticed. The last thing I need is a romance."

Jackson grunted in agreement. "Yeah, and don't I know it. If I get any more shipments of sod and fertilizer, I'll have to change the name from Valley Hardware to Valley Weed n' Seed."

Seth frowned, then asked, "When's the last time you went out on a date, boy?" He'd been so worried about what the responsibilities of running the store had done to him that he hadn't given a thought to what it was doing to Jackson. Jackson was only a year younger, but Seth felt ten years older sometimes.

"I don't remember, and it's too depressing to think about so get your mind back on manure."

Both men turned their attention to business for awhile, unloading the fertilizer truck in companionable silence. It had always been this way with them, feeling more like brothers than cousins, but as close as they were, they didn't have the same goals in life. Jackson was perfectly content to live out his days right here in Ruby Valley, smothered by the attention of family and friends, while Seth wanted to get away from it all and find a place where family interference didn't reach.

When the wooden pallet was full, Seth climbed onto the forklift, picked up the pallet, and drove it into the storeroom, where he stacked it against the wall. As he drove back out toward the loading area, winding his way through the building his family had built, the business that had been his father's dream, the feeling struck anew: he had to go. It had played like a theme song throughout his life, more often in recent years. He'd never gotten on well with his dad and had waited and planned for the day he'd be free to follow his own dreams.

He and Charlie had spent years back in high school and college planning their construction business, which they'd hoped to start much sooner than this, but his father's first heart attack had caused what was supposed to be a temporary postponement. Seth had just graduated from college when the call came. He was needed at home while his father healed, just until his dad could get back on his feet. But it had never happened. The second heart attack, just six months later, had killed him. Seth had assumed his father's role in the business, and two years later, Jackson's father had retired, handing over the reins to Jackson, who hadn't been quite ready to take them. Somehow, Seth had been saddled with the responsibilities of the whole place and couldn't bring himself to leave Jackson on his own, even when Elizabeth finally settled down and came on board as bookkeeper. Until now.

He glanced over at his cousin who'd just hefted another sack over his shoulder, and felt a certain amount of pride. Jackson had come a long way in a short time and was ready to make it on his own. He'd be around to look after Liz and Aunt Maude if needed, but Seth didn't think that would be all that often anymore. Liz had mellowed and was staying out of trouble nowadays, and Aunt Maude was content running everyone's lives. It was time to cut the family cord and let everyone rise to their full potential. He'd fulfilled every promise his father and life had wrenched out of him and then some.

Come September he'd be in Charlotte with Charlie, who'd already gotten the business up and running. There was a construction boom going on there, in spite of a slumping economy, and the city was ripe for the plucking. He planned on catching the wave and riding it as long as it lasted, but he'd promised his cousins he'd wait until after their busy summer season. Most of the seasonal residents would pack up their summer homes and head back to Florida for the winter, so business would slack off by then.

Gillian was from Florida, he remembered her saying, but she wouldn't be going back this fall. She'd be staying right here in Ruby Valley if her business succeeded. That pleased him, though he couldn't say why. He wouldn't be here then anyway.

"Hey, get your mind back on business." Jackson tossed him the last bag off the truck, nearly knocking him off balance. "You've done enough daydreaming."

"Just thinking about September."

"Really?" His cousin looked doubtful. "Usually you have this blissful look on your face when you're thinking about going to Charlotte."

Seth set the bag on the pallet at his feet and wiped at the sweat on his brow with the back of his work glove. He looked up at Jackson, curious. "What look did I have instead?"

"I don't know. Worry, maybe. Probably worked too hard out in the heat today." Jackson stopped and wiped the sweat off his own forehead. "It's hot as hell out here."

"Yeah, that's probably it. I'm just tired," Seth reassured himself. Charlotte was his dream and nothing—not family, not business, not even a gorgeous redhead who stirred his blood—was going to stand in his way.

With the last of the bags unloaded, he gave a wave to Jackson and left the store for the night, but he didn't head for home. Instead, he turned his pickup onto the highway and headed back out toward his current job at the Stinson place. If he was going to start on Gillian's place by the next week, he was going to have to work double-time on this one. It was going to take a miracle to get her ready to open on schedule, and he wasn't convinced she could make a go of it even if she got it reopened, but if it would help her achieve her dream, he was willing to try. He was a man who believed in dreams.

Later that night, as he passed her place on the way to his own, he couldn't help thinking about Gillian. What did she think she was doing coming back to the valley after all those years away and buying a dump like the Keeneys' place? What did Ruby Valley have to offer her now?

Only time would tell, he figured, turning his attention to the twisting mountain road that led to his cabin. He wouldn't waste any more time thinking about her tonight. She'd been gone more than a decade. What was there to think about?

But later, after a tall, cold beer and long, hot shower, he found sleep elusive as he tossed and turned, remembering a pretty, sad-eyed girl and wondering what kind of woman she had become.

Chapter Three

Gillian let the parlor curtain flutter back into place and checked her watch again. It was almost eight. Almost time for Seth to arrive for his first day on the job.

Forcing herself away from the window, she walked back to the kitchen to check on the coffee she had brewing and stopped to check her appearance in the antique tiger oak-framed mirror she'd hung in the hallway. She wanted to look professional for this meeting. Seth had seen her for the first time as a grown-up with bed head and no makeup, and she wanted to make a different kind of impression today—that of a competent businesswoman. Long gone was that rough and tumble tomboy she used to be. It was important that he know.

In the three weeks she'd been back in the valley she felt she'd made some serious headway in getting the shop ready for business. Seth had sent his plumber friend out to check on things, and he'd temporarily fixed her pipes right and tight. Later, when she had the funds, she could have the plumbing modernized. Hopefully it wouldn't take long to operate in the black since she was running seriously low on cash. She'd used her trust-fund money, left to her upon her father's death, to buy the shop, but it was her personal savings she was dipping into to make the necessary improvements. And she had to eat. When she'd said as much to Seth, she hadn't been joking.

Stepping into her office, which was really a storage closet tucked beneath the stairs, she booted up her computer so she could work on her inventory list while she waited. It was tedious work and not her favorite part of running an antique business, but it was vital for survival. One day, once the shop was seeing success, she'd hire someone to do it, but for now she was on her own. Since the Keeney brothers hadn't kept any kind of inventory records, it was a monumental but necessary task.

Tires crunching on gravel pulled Gillian from her thoughts and she went to look out the front window again. Seth's truck was coming up the drive. A quick glance at her watch told her he was right on time.

"Good morning, come on in," she chirped brightly as she opened the door. She was struck again by his rugged good looks. He certainly wasn't hard on the eyes. "I've got some coffee brewing in the kitchen if you'd like some before you get started."

Seth smiled warmly, wiped his feet on her pretty sunflower doormat, and walked into the parlor where he set his toolbox on the floor. "I was kind of hoping I'd get here early enough to roust you out of bed again," he teased, grinning wickedly. "I'll make sure I get here a little earlier tomorrow."

"Good luck," she teased back, turning to lead the way to the kitchen, leaving him to follow or not. "I'm up most mornings before six for my run. You just caught me on an off day last time."

He followed her into the kitchen. "You're a morning person then. Where do you run?"

"North on Highway Twenty-eight to the swinging bridge," she answered. "The sunrise is breathtaking from out there."

"I'm surprised I didn't see you this morning on the way into town. I live out that way up in the foothills, a few miles past your folks' old place."

Her heart tightened a bit at the mention of her childhood home. She walked over to the coffeemaker and reached for the carafe, then glanced over her shoulder to find him leaning in the doorway. "Have a seat if you'd like," she said, pouring two cups of steaming coffee into oversized ceramic mugs.

Seth continued to lean lazily against the door frame, overwhelming the tiny kitchen. He made no move to sit down as she'd asked, so she took his coffee to him where he stood. "Cream, sugar?" she asked, though she remembered he'd taken it black the other day.

"No thanks." As he reached out to take the cup she offered, his fingers brushed hers and she jolted slightly at the sensation, sloshing a bit of coffee on his hand.

"Oh, I'm sorry, let me get you a napkin. Do you need some ice?"

"I'm okay," he said, wiping his hand on his old, worn jeans, then taking a sip from the cup. "Have you been out to see it yet?"

"The house?" She'd been planning on it but simply hadn't had the guts to do it yet. Just like she hadn't been to the cemetery to put flowers on her father's grave. There were just too many questions left unanswered, like why he'd never tried to see her or even call her after her mother had taken her away. Ruefully, she shook her head and stirred sugar into her coffee, then leaned against the counter and met his eyes. "Does she still live there?"

His gaze was speculative, as though trying to discern her motives for asking, and Gillian shifted her eyes upward to look at the cobwebs dangling in the corner above his head. "Patty. She's a nice woman. Did you ever meet her?"

Gillian shook her head. "I never talked to Daddy once

we left here. No letters. No phone calls. No birthday cards. I don't even know what she looks like."

"She's pretty and very nice. Not much older than you. I think she'd like to meet you."

Seth walked across to Gillian and leaned against the counter next to her, not close enough to touch but close enough for her to feel his presence. If she closed her eyes she'd still sense his nearness.

"You want me to give her a call for you and sort of break the ice?"

Her heart fluttered like a hummingbird's wings at the thought. "I'll do it when I'm ready, but thanks for offering. I'm sure she knows I'm here. Maybe she'll come by to see me."

Seth reached out and touched her arm as she started to move away. "Don't wait too long, okay?" he coaxed. "I'd hate to see either one of you hurt by careless gossip, and if folks sense that you're afraid to see her then they'll assume . . ."

She pulled her arm away and planted her hands on her hips. "I'm not afraid of meeting her. I just don't have time right now. I've got a shop to open and not much time to do that. Besides, it's nobody's business but mine whether I'm planning on meeting her or not, and you can make sure you tell that to anyone who asks, since you seem to be so worried about it."

Seth merely shrugged. "You're right. It *is* your business, but there are some things you should know, and I think you'd rather hear them straight from her than from someone else. The folks around here sort of believe that everybody's business *is* everybody's business. They like to take care of their own."

He set his nearly full cup of coffee on the counter, then walked past her toward the hallway that led back to the parlor. "By the way, you can expect a visit from Elizabeth in the next few days. She's about as curious as a cat about you, and I won't dangle any details for her to bat around. You've made it clear that your business is your business."

"Thanks for the warning, but it's a little too late. She's already called to invite me to Fiddlin' on the Square on Saturday night. I hear there'll be some killer cloggers there."

"You're not going, are you?"

She caught the warning note in his voice and bristled. She'd always hated being told what to do. "Why shouldn't I?"

"Well for one thing, you might as well climb on top of the gazebo roof down at the town square, grab a bullhorn, and tell the good folks of Ruby Valley every personal detail about yourself because that's exactly what's going to happen if you hang around with Elizabeth. Then you'll see whose business your business really is."

Gillian sipped from her cup and eyed him thoughtfully over the rim. "You two aren't any closer than you used to be, are you? How do you survive in business together?"

"I love my cousin, but I'm not blind to her faults. You shouldn't be either. Thanks for the coffee. I've got work to do," he said, then disappeared down the hallway, leaving Gillian alone in the kitchen to contemplate his advice.

Should she heed it? She and Elizabeth had never been friends, though they'd been thrown together often enough as children since they'd been the same age and in many of the same classes in school and the youth group at church. Elizabeth had been too prissy and sure of herself for Gillian's tastes, and Gillian had been too much of a tomboy for Elizabeth and her friends.

But still, people change with time and maturity, don't they? Look at me. I'm not the scruffy little kid I used to be. Maybe Elizabeth's not the snotty little girl she used to be. It was nice of Elizabeth to ask her along to the Saturday night festival, no matter what her motive, and Gillian was determined to go. It would be a good way to meet new people and maybe reacquaint herself with some old friends.

And what about Patricia Guy? nagged a little voice as she walked to her office beneath the stairs and started in on the inventory lists again. *Seth's right about that one.* She'd better make some sort of overture toward her before people made up stories about why they hadn't yet met. She'd planned on going out to the house when she had time, but what in the world would she say to the woman? "Hi, I'm the stepdaughter you never met. I just moved back to town, but if that makes you at all uncomfortable, just ignore my presence." Or how about, "Hey, I was really hurt and angry when my father married you, but I think I'm ready to move past the resentment. What do you say? Think we could go visit his grave together?"

The sound of footsteps descending the stairs above her drew her attention and she listened to see where Seth was going. The front door opened and closed and she let out the breath she hadn't been aware she was holding.

It was strange having Seth back in her life, especially as an employee of sorts. He'd been her first crush, for goodness' sake. Before he lobbed that rock at her head, he'd been the one she'd set her eyes on. They'd had so much in common, and he'd understood her better than just about anyone around. In her youthful heart, he'd been the perfect boy for her. Until he'd run away and clobbered her with a rock.

He'd been the object of a young innocent's fantasies back then, but she wasn't delusional anymore. There wasn't anything magical about him, nothing out of the ordinary to make him stand out above the rest. He didn't have a thing that any other red-blooded male didn't have. As a mature, grown woman who knew far better than to waste dreams on the opposite sex, she could see him for what he actually was, and he was just a man.

An attractive, unattached, available man. He hadn't said

as much, but Darcy down at the Piggly Wiggly had filled her in. He used to be quite the stud, according to the gabby grocery-store cashier, but for the past year or so, he'd been going it alone. And that made him tempting.

Business before pleasure, she reminded herself as she turned her attention back to her computer screen and picked up where she'd left off, glad she wasn't a love-struck pre-teen anymore.

As she worked, she half-listened for the sound of the front door opening, then sighed when it did, and couldn't help but follow the sound of his footsteps as he climbed the rickety stairs again. She mentally chastised herself for allowing herself to be so distracted. What was wrong with her? Hopefully a night out with Elizabeth would be just the diversion she needed. It had been too long since she'd been out to socialize, and even longer since she'd had a date with a handsome man. Maybe Elizabeth could introduce her to someone so her social life could pick up after her shop opened.

But not Seth, she assured herself. Theirs was just a business relationship.

He popped his head in the doorway as though her very thoughts had summoned him. "What do you have planned for lunch today?"

Her stomach jumped. Seth was asking her to lunch? For the life of her, she couldn't remember what she'd planned on doing for lunch. Had she planned on doing anything? "I . . . um, I'm just going to fix myself a sandwich and have it here."

He'd flustered her and he knew it. She could tell by the wicked little light in his eyes, and she wished she'd come up with something brilliant to tell him like, "I don't eat with the hired help," or "I have a previous engagement, thank you for asking." Now he'd know she was free and really had no good excuse for turning him down.

"Good. You can make one for me too, if you don't mind.

I don't want to take the time to drive into town since we're on such a tight schedule, and I forgot to pack one today." He winked at her, his grin spreading nearly from ear to ear, like a mischievous little imp.

Her brows came down over narrowed eyes. "Turkey."

"Pardon me?" His own eyes narrowed just the slightest bit, his smile drooping, as he questioned what he'd just heard.

She smiled innocently. "Turkey, as in turkey sandwich. Is that okay with you, or do you prefer ham?"

His lopsided grin dimpled one cheek, rattling her nerves. "That'll be just fine, thank you. And some iced tea with lemon, if you have it. Sweetened."

She wanted to tell him what he could do with his sweetened tea, but he was gone and bounding back up the stairs before she could come up with a suitable suggestion. He'd probably have enjoyed anything she could have come up with anyway, and then offered some suggestions of his own.

Boy, he was a charmer with just the right amount of scoundrel thrown in. Where was that sweet, quiet boy she'd so idolized, and what had she gotten herself into when she'd hired him to do the renovations? She didn't know how in the world she was going to survive working this closely with him for the next thirty days, but she was sure of one thing: it was going to be one very, very long month.

Chapter Four

Saturday night rolled around much faster than Gillian had thought it would, and as she put the finishing touches on her makeup she found herself eagerly anticipating the evening with Elizabeth. She needed a break from business in the worst way. It was time to get out and meet some new people; the only person she'd spent any time getting to know was Seth.

They'd gotten into the habit of sharing lunch together beneath the willow tree each day, and she'd learned about what she'd come to think of as "the lost years" of his life.

His father's death, then his mother's a few years later, had taken their toll on him over the years though he downplayed it, and her heart went out to him. She knew how wrenching it was to lose a parent. She found herself opening up and telling him about her mother, Anita, and her marriage to Joe, who'd turned out to be a surprisingly good stepfather for a lonely girl whose mother expected too much from her in exchange for so very little. Seth had listened until she'd run out of things to say, and instead of the pity she'd feared, she'd seen admiration in his eyes. A friendship, of sorts, had been forged.

A glance at her watch confirmed it was nearly six, so

she quickly checked her appearance in the bathroom mirror and was satisfied with what she saw. The evening was too hot for jeans, so she'd chosen a short faded denim skirt and a sleeveless Indian print cotton blouse to wear with comfy Birkenstock sandals. With a last little fluff of her hair, she deemed herself ready to go and walked across the lawn to the shop's front porch to wait for Elizabeth to pick her up.

Seth's truck parked in front of the shop surprised her. He'd left hours before to do some odd jobs for another customer who'd been moved to the back burner. What was he doing back? She tried the front door, found it opened, and stepped inside.

"Seth?" she called into the darkened house, but received no answer. She flipped on the parlor light and closed the door behind her. "Seth?" she called up the stairs.

When she still heard nothing, she went up to investigate, but he wasn't there. Foiled, she went back downstairs to check the kitchen and nearly had the life scared out of her when Seth suddenly appeared in the doorway.

"I thought you'd already gone," he said, then took in her appearance and whistled appreciatively.

She took a breath and tried to settle her suddenly skittish nerves as they faced each other. "Elizabeth's picking me up any minute now. Why didn't you answer when I called?"

"Guess I didn't hear you. I was down in the basement hanging a light over your work area. It's dark down there, but at least it's cooler than the rest of the place. I put in florescent so it won't get too hot for you. I checked the boards on the staircase too, to make sure you're not going to break your neck falling through."

It was so sweet of him to think of things like that, and he was constantly doing it. Without giving it a thought, she reached up and gave him a hug, then quickly stepped away, hoping she hadn't overstepped her bounds. She was suddenly absurdly aware of her hands and, not knowing what to do with them, clasped them in front of her. "When I saw your truck, I figured you'd come back," she said, stating the obvious and feeling ridiculous for having done so.

"Stands to reason," he agreed, that dratted sparkle in his eyes again, letting her know he was aware of her discomfort and thoroughly enjoying it. It was like a game of cat and mouse, and he was winning at the moment.

"So I came to find you," she explained unnecessarily, wondering if he knew his eyes were like warm chocolate flecked with golden honey, deciding he probably did and used it to his advantage whenever possible.

"Do you need something?" he asked.

"Um, no, I . . ." she stammered, embarrassed, and stepped back a good foot toward safety. It would be easy to make a fool out of herself over this man. "I was just checking to make sure you were alright. I didn't expect you to come back tonight."

He cocked his head to one side and raised an eyebrow that seemed to mock her. "You were worried about me? Afraid I'd hammer my thumb or step on a nail?"

"No, I just wondered why you came back. You've been working so hard all week, and I thought you'd gone for the day. I didn't expect you to be here, that's all," she finished lamely.

A blush stole across her cheeks as a slow smile spread across his lips. He knew why she'd come. She'd wanted an excuse to see him, and he knew it. And even though she *knew* he knew, she still couldn't bring herself to turn and leave. In fact, she suddenly wondered what it would be like to kiss him.

Her heart pounded in her ears as she contemplated the pros and cons of such a move, but the sound of a horn brought her back to reality before she could say or do anything foolish. "That's Elizabeth," she said unnecessarily, feeling decidedly disappointed.

"You'd better get going then," he said, his eyes trapping

hers and holding on tenaciously. It was as though he held some power over her.

She nodded, but didn't move, unwilling to break the eye contact just yet. For just another moment, she wanted to savor him like a piece of art or a fine wine—bold, woodsy, and well-aged.

The horn sounded again more insistently and, regretfully, she turned and left the shop and Seth behind. Even more regretful was the fact that he let her go. If Elizabeth had arrived just five minutes later, what might have happened? "See you Monday," she called over her shoulder.

"Probably sooner than that," he called back. "I'll be at the square with Jackson later on. We play a mean duet on the harmonica."

Harmonica? Seth Connor plays the harmonica? She tried to imagine a visual of Seth playing like a good ol' boy, but the thought was too ridiculous. He had to be teasing her.

With a light step and a smile, she walked out to meet Elizabeth, who was waiting in the car. She wasn't sure what had happened back there with Seth, but it intrigued her. Something new was definitely coming around the bend.

"Hey." Elizabeth's smile was bright and welcoming as Gillian slid into the passenger seat of the Corolla.

"Hi," Gillian said in return. "Thanks for inviting me to come along."

Elizabeth backed out of the drive and turned the car toward town. "My pleasure. I wanted to welcome you back, find out how you've been and all that. I wasn't sure you'd come," she said honestly.

Gillian wondered how much to divulge, then decided on the truth. "I almost didn't. I wasn't sure why you invited me, to tell you the truth."

Elizabeth nodded. "We weren't the best of friends as

kids, were we? But there's no reason we can't be friends now. I'll bet Seth warned you not to come, didn't he?"

Gillian studied the petite woman who was so like Seth with her dark beauty. Her eyes were the same chocolate brown as Seth's and fringed with thick black lashes. She doubted Elizabeth even had to bother with mascara, but based on her perfectly lined lips and manicured nails, she figured she probably did anyway. She wondered how Elizabeth would take it if she knew Seth *had* warned her?

"He did, didn't he?" Elizabeth prodded.

"Maybe a little," she hedged, then relaxed when Elizabeth simply flashed a smile. She could see she wasn't offended.

"Seth's decided to take you under his wing of protection, so to speak, to keep the grapevine gossip to a minimum. He's probably trembling in his boots with worry that I'm tape-recording everything you say to broadcast on the local radio station, WRVT. That's what the RVT stands for you know. Ruby Valley Talks."

Gillian laughed, then sobered. "You're not, are you?"

"No, but I'll probably spill a few beans at Fancy Fingers when I have my nails done on Tuesday so just let me know what's okay to tell and what's not."

Gillian couldn't ask for more than that, she supposed. "I'm not sure there's much to say that anyone would be interested in hearing. Maybe I should take Seth's advice and do my own storytelling. I could just hand out leaflets or something and then everyone's curiosity would be satisfied."

"Yeah, but they wouldn't have nearly as much fun. It's amazing how the tiniest little things can become really big deals to the folks around here. Especially dark family secrets."

"Believe me when I tell you there are no dark secrets lingering in my past. I'm afraid people are going to have to be disappointed with my life story."

Elizabeth shot Gillian a look of sympathy, then turned her eyes back to the twisting road. "You'd better make something up to satisfy them then, because if you don't, they will."

Gillian laughed. Elizabeth made it sound so serious, but it couldn't be all that bad. She hoped. "Tell me about to-night," she said in an effort to change the subject. "Who's playing?"

"Well, you probably remember Mr. Holmes from when we were kids. He's still playing the fiddle like nobody's business. There's a clogging group from over in Highlands, like I already told you, and then the locals just jam together like they always do. Things haven't changed that much since you lived here."

Gillian was glad to hear it. She'd always remembered her childhood hometown as being a warm, friendly place where people waved hello and you knew your neighbors. When the tourists were in town, business boomed and when they went back home, their community was quiet and cozy. She hoped it was just the way she remembered it and couldn't wait to find out if it was. "Seth said he and Jackson will be playing later."

Elizabeth's eyebrows shot to the top of her forehead, and she glanced over with a disbelieving look. "He did? Good Lord, I wonder what brought that on."

Gillian was convinced that Seth had been teasing her after all. Why else would his cousin look so surprised?

They chatted about the community the rest of the way into town, and within fifteen minutes or so Elizabeth pulled into the First Methodist Church lot to park. She grabbed a couple of lounge chairs from the trunk and handed one to Gillian, then led the way to the grassy area surrounding the gazebo in the square. The music had already started, and sure enough, Mr. Holmes, a bit more gray and a lot more stooped than Gillian recalled, was fiddling away.

A few people called to Elizabeth once they were settled

and some came to visit and introduce themselves to Gillian, then went on their way with a promise to visit her shop when it opened. Gillian was pleased to find the people as friendly as she remembered, and, feeling thoroughly satisfied with her first social outing, sat back and enjoyed the festivities.

After an hour she found her thoughts drifting to Seth and wondered when he'd arrive. She scanned the crowd, which was much thicker than before, but couldn't find him. A feeling akin to disappointment settled in her stomach.

Luckily, Elizabeth provided plenty of distraction by leaning over every few minutes and pointing out someone new to Gillian. "That's Marilee Martin over there, only she's Marilee Cooper now. She married the Cooper boy who was a couple of years older than Seth. There's Keith Sutherland with his second wife, Deborah. He married some girl he met at college, but she wasn't cut out for small-town life like we were. She left him for a used-car salesman from Miami, I heard, and hasn't been back since."

"Is there anything you don't know about these people?" Seth had been right about one thing. Elizabeth loved gossip.

"There are a few I'm still working on." She sent Gillian a sidelong glance and grinned, making Gillian feel a bit like a canary sitting next to a very hungry cat. "Don't worry, I promised I won't tell anything you don't want me to, and I won't."

Gillian sincerely wanted to believe that but doubted she should. Elizabeth was just enjoying herself too much to make her think she'd show any restraint, no matter what the circumstances.

"Don't believe a word she says, Gillian. The town will know everything you've said by sunset tomorrow. Now come dance with me." Seth appeared from behind them, making her heart leap into her throat. He was clean-shaven, had changed into jeans and a fresh T-shirt, and looked just as delicious as he had all scruffy from a day of labor. She wondered if he smelled as delicious too.

Without a second thought, she took the hand he offered and let him lead her to the dancing area, though she hadn't a clue how to dance to a fiddle. The other couples were twirling around in well-practiced steps she remembered seeing as a child, but she'd never had the opportunity to learn. She looked at Seth for guidance and was relieved when he simply took her in his arms and swayed her gently to the music.

Her senses took over as she closed her eyes and enjoyed the warmth of his arms around her. She inhaled softly and found his clean scent tantalizing. His arms were warm and solid, yet held her gently as they moved in time with the strains of the fiddle. What would it be like, she wondered, to take one step closer. Would his arms tighten around her, holding her there, or would he step back, putting distance between them?

She opened her eyes and was surprised to see him staring at her. Her breath caught in her throat, and she wondered if he'd somehow read her mind when he pulled her just the slightest bit closer, his arms wrapping securely around her.

"Where were you just now?" he asked, his breath fanning across her cheek, making her stomach flutter.

"Just enjoying the dance," she answered softly, wondering if he could hear the lie in her voice, hoping he wouldn't pursue it if he did.

He continued to probe her eyes with his own, as though searching for the truth, but he didn't push it. Instead, he slid a hand up her back to her neck and gently pulled her even closer until her temple rested against his jaw. "As soon as Jackson gets here, we're going to play a few tunes with the guys in the band," he whispered in her ear, sending delicious little shivers skittering down her neck like water dancing across a hot skillet. "Will you stick around and listen?"

Gillian chuckled. "I wouldn't miss you playing the harmonica for anything in the world."

"Go ahead and laugh all you want, but you'll be apologizing for it later," Seth retorted teasingly. "I play a mean harmonica."

Gillian couldn't help the little snort that escaped when she laughed, and was surprised when Seth wrapped her in a bear hug and nuzzled her neck, making her laugh even harder as she tried to pull away. "That's just the cutest thing I've ever heard, Gillian. I'll have to find more ways to make you laugh."

Then, too soon the dance was over, and he led her back to her chair long before she was ready to go. With a promise to see her later, he disappeared into the thickening crowd, leaving her alone with Elizabeth once again.

"Wow," Elizabeth said. "I haven't seen Seth like that in a long time."

Gillian's curiosity was piqued. "Like what?"

"Lighthearted, carefree. I don't know . . . happy, I guess. He used to date as often as I do, and that's a lot, but he hasn't been out in nearly a year now. I swear the only thing that makes him happy nowadays is thinking of Charlotte."

Charlotte? She felt a prick of jealousy, then put it in perspective and called herself a fool. It could be his dog for all she knew. What difference should it make to her anyway?

"Elizabeth, introduce me to your friend."

Gillian's questions were shelved for the moment with the untimely arrival of Seth's Aunt Maude. She looked older, of course, but Gillian recognized her right off. "I'm Gillian Guy, Mrs. Strickland," she said, extending her hand.

The older woman took her hand and squeezed it warmly, holding it for a moment as she examined Gillian's face. "Frank and Anita Guy's daughter. I remember when you were just a girl. We're neighbors, you know."

Gillian was surprised to hear that. There was only one

other house within walking distance and it was a couple of lots away from hers, but since it was mostly obscured by trees, she hadn't seen much activity over there and had thought maybe it was vacant. "Where do you live?" she asked, just to make sure she had the right place.

"Right next door. I'm surprised Seth didn't tell you. I've seen his truck over at your place all week long, and I've been curious about what he's been up to."

"Why don't you come on over on Monday and take a look around? Seth's taking care of some maintenance issues while I clean up the furniture and take inventory. I'm afraid it's still a mess inside, but I'm working on it piece by piece."

Maude frowned. "The Keeney brothers never lifted a hand around that place in all the years they owned it. I thought it would fall down around their ears one day. When Bill died, I wondered what Edward would do, but I never dreamed he'd actually sell the place lock, stock, and barrel."

Gillian grimaced, then laughed. "Barrels, plural. Lots of barrels, boxes, trunks . . . you name it, it's there."

"Elizabeth says you're trying to get the place opened up by the end of June. That's just a month away. Are you going to be able to manage it by yourself?"

Gillian cast a baleful glance toward Elizabeth, who was suddenly very interested in her manicure. "I'm alone in this endeavor, but I'm up to the task."

Mrs. Strickland smiled. "If you'd like some help, I'm available most days. I come into town for my hair appointment and grocery shopping every Tuesday, and Sundays I'm at church, but I'm free the other days."

Gillian was touched. "That's such a kind offer, but I wouldn't be able to pay you for your time. I'm just going it alone until I can afford to hire some help. I'm afraid it'll be awhile."

"You don't have to pay me. That's what neighbors do

for each other around here. Now, I'm going to go sit down and enjoy the music for awhile, then I'm taking these weary bones home to bed. I'll see you Monday."

"Thank you so much. I guess I'll see you then," Gillian called as she watched the older woman walk away. "Isn't that nice?"

Elizabeth's eyes were wide. "Nice? Wait until Seth finds out she's going to be working under the same roof as him for the next month."

"What's wrong with that?"

"Aunt Maude is just about the bossiest, nosiest person in the entire valley. She's Aunt Grace's sister and never had children of her own, so she just adopted everyone else's. She's not even my aunt, but she calls me almost every day to check on me and find out who I'm going out with. When my mother died, she wanted to raise me. Thank heaven my father said no. I don't think either one of us could have survived the experience. We'd have done each other in."

Gillian laughed. "She doesn't seem that bad."

"You can do what you want, but you'll find out the hard way if you let her help you for the next month," Elizabeth warned, then stood up and stretched like a cat. "I'm going to go wander around and see what I can stir up. It's a little too boring around here for my tastes. You want to come along?"

Gillian shook her head. "I think I'll take a little walk down Main Street and see how much it's changed. Maybe I'll get an ice cream cone or some cotton candy on my way back. Would you like some? My treat."

"I'll get something later. Right now, I have my eye on Tom Hawkins over there," she said, pointing a slender finger across to the other side of the street. "I want to dance."

Gillian watched as Elizabeth sashayed across the street and took the man by the hand. Sure enough, he popped right up and followed her like a puppy on a leash. The petite woman oozed self-confidence, and she wondered what it would be like to be as sure of herself as Elizabeth seemed to be. What would it be like to walk right up to a man and kiss him, just to see what it felt like?

Seth popped into her mind, and she laughed at herself. He was attractive and tempting, and it had been heaven dancing with him, but she didn't plan on kissing him, or anyone else, anytime soon.

Hoping to get her mind off that particular train of thought, she set off down Main Street in the opposite direction of the crowd to see what had changed over the past fifteen years. The street was lined with the same red brick buildings she remembered, and if she didn't read any of the signs on the storefronts, she could almost believe she'd never been away and things were just the same. But the signs weren't the same as they had been. They'd changed with the times, just as she had. She suddenly felt alone and just the tiniest bit fearful.

When she'd dreamed of returning, she hadn't considered the changes that had taken place in Ruby Valley while she'd been gone. She hadn't realized how much time and effort it would take to get to know people, even in a small town. True friendships didn't just happen, they had to be cultivated and nurtured. How would she have the time to do that if she was busy running a store on the outskirts of town? For the first time in her life, she was really and truly on her own.

Of course, there was Patricia Guy, her father's widow, but that could prove to be awkward. What if Patricia didn't want to meet her? That would make things uncomfortable in the future if they were both living in the same town, doing everything possible to avoid contact with each other. Why hadn't she considered that before, and maybe written a letter to let her know she was coming?

And then there was Seth. She certainly hadn't anticipated the changes she'd found in him. She remembered the boy, and liked the man he'd turned into. He was capable and kind, fun and attractive. And a really good dancer. She stopped walking for a moment and touched a finger to her lips, wondering again how it would feel to kiss him.

Shaking herself from her foolish daydreams, she strolled further down the empty sidewalk past the closed tourist shops and focused again on the sights around her. She couldn't find anything remotely familiar. The pet shop was gone and Earl's Barbershop was now called Cassandra's Day Spa. Even the drugstore had been bought out by a national chain. Was it too much to ask for just one thing to have stayed the same?

A little disillusioned, she contemplated turning back toward the square, but she wasn't yet ready to rejoin the festivities, so she turned the corner instead and found herself face-to-face with Valley Hardware, Seth's business. It hadn't changed a bit. Its concrete block walls were the same tan, its trim the same brown. The sign over the door looked like the original, though she was sure it must have been replaced or repaired at some point in its existence.

She'd been in that store many times with her father getting nails or screws, and even once, a new lawnmower. Her heart softened at the memory and she was a girl once again. Her dad would hold her hand in his large, warm one until Seth's dad would walk over and the men would talk hardware. Then, temporarily forgotten, she'd slip away to look for Seth. Those had been simple times. Things just weren't that simple anymore.

A movement caught her eye, and she was surprised to see Seth walk out of the store as though her thoughts had conjured him up. He locked the door, then turned and looked directly at Gillian where she was standing across the street. She felt like a voyeur who'd been caught spying. Too late, she wished she'd turned back when she'd had the chance, but there was nothing she could do about it now. She only hoped he wouldn't think she'd been looking for him.

He walked across the deserted street, and as he came toward her, her heart did a little dance. She couldn't help thinking of how he'd looked, all rough and work-worn, standing in her kitchen earlier. Every sense she possessed had been drawn to him then, again when they'd danced, and now as well. She wasn't sure how it had happened in just one short week, but she was definitely attracted to the man.

So what was she going to do about it? *Run,* her mind warned, *and fast!* But her feet weren't listening.

"Gillian, what are you doing way down here?" he asked as he approached, his dark eyes crinkling with a smile. "No, don't tell me, let me guess. The Georgia Cloggers got started and scared you away."

He had a way of making her smile, and she wondered if he was always this charming, or if she was special. "I just wanted to take a look around, see if I recognized anything on Main Street."

He shook his head. "Not likely. Shops come and go around here on a pretty regular basis. It's not like when we were kids and things never changed."

"The hardware store hasn't changed," she commented, then wondered aloud, "Why is that? You never wanted to modernize it?"

Seth shrugged and looked back over his shoulder at the building in question. "It works the way it is."

"That's good. Hey, I thought you were going to play your mean harmonica. You're not hiding out down here to avoid it are you?"

He laughed, put an arm around her shoulders, and turned her back in the direction from which she'd just come. Then, very casually, he let his hand slip around her waist and drew her closer. "I recognize doubt when I hear it. You think I'm going to stink."

Indulging in the moment, she slipped her own arm around his waist and let it rest as casually as possible against the small of his back. "I'm not convinced yet that you're really going to play at all. Now, tell me. Why were you down at the store when you should be enjoying the evening?"

"I've got a lot to do and not enough hours in the day to do it all. There's this pushy client who's insisting on getting two months' worth of work out of me in just a few short weeks, so I'm working overtime on some other stuff."

She knew he was teasing, but she was instantly contrite. "You're working late at the store because of me? That's why you came back to work at my place, isn't it? I had no idea. I guess I thought you just handled one job at a time, but Seth, if you can't do the work, just say so and I'll . . ."

He pressed his fingers against her mouth, effectively staunching the flow of words. They came to a standstill on the sidewalk and stood staring at each other. She parted her lips and let out a trembly little sigh.

His warm, dark eyes delved into hers, searching for something, though for what she couldn't be sure because she knew she had no answers to any questions he might ask. Then, she felt his arm drawing her closer and knew he was going to kiss her.

With true regret, she slipped out of his arms and set her feet back in motion walking up the street, chatting as though nothing of importance had nearly transpired be-tween them. "I noticed that Earl's Barber Shop isn't around anymore. Did he retire or is he calling himself Cassandra nowadays? And whatever happened to the pet store that used to be on the corner over there? Pets never go out of style, so you'd think they'd have stuck it out," she babbled, trying to keep her mouth occupied with something other than kissing Seth.

If he wondered if she'd gone crazy, he didn't comment on it. To her relief, he fell into step beside her, letting her ramble as she would, and soon they were back at the lounge chairs. Gillian was grateful to be able to have a seat; her legs were terribly unsteady.

"I'm going to go find Jackson," Seth said easily, "and see what we can do to change your misconceptions about harmonicas. You'll stay and listen?"

She promised she would, and then he was gone, disappearing once more into the crowd.

Before Gillian could steady her runaway heart, Elizabeth slipped back into her chair looking winded and happy. "Get ready for a show. Seth and Jackson really rock the place and they haven't played for a long, long time now. I don't think they played even once last summer, and this is the first time this season. It should be good."

Elizabeth's enthusiasm was contagious and Gillian found herself caught up in it. She couldn't wait to hear him play. "That's what Seth promised."

"They're getting set up right now. It should only be a few more minutes. Listen, I'm going to go see if I can give them a hand, okay?"

"Sure." Gillian watched Elizabeth walk to the gazebo and sidle up to one of the guys setting up the sound system. She wasn't surprised that Elizabeth didn't lift a hand to help since it was obvious that she'd gone over just to flirt. With fascination, she watched Elizabeth totally distract the man until he was doing more talking than setting up. Finally, one of the other guys shooed them out of the way, and Gillian smiled. Watching Elizabeth was like watching art in motion, and she envied her once again. It was obvious she had the ability to keep things light and carefree where men were concerned. It used to be as easy as that for Gillian, but she didn't think she could manage it with Seth. There was just something different about him.

Finally, the system was ready to go and Seth and Jackson took the stage, but there wasn't a harmonica in sight. Seth played an electric guitar while Jackson played the keyboard, and their sound was amazing. They played everything from country to rock and roll, Garth Brooks to Elton John, and the place was hopping. Finally, they wrapped it all up with a final song, and to Gillian's delight, they both pulled harmonicas out of their shirt pockets and played an amazingly complex tune to the rousing cheers of the community around them. Seth was every bit as talented as he'd promised and just full of surprises. Gillian was more than impressed.

With the show over, folks started packing up to head for home, and Elizabeth finally reappeared with her friend in tow. "Gillian, I'm going to go for an ice cream soda with Hank. Do you want to come along?"

Gillian suddenly felt like a third wheel, so she shook her head. "I'm really beat. Do you think you could drop me off first? I've got to get an early start at the shop tomorrow."

"I thought you'd say that, so I asked Seth to take you home since it's on his way. He'll be over to get you in a few minutes." Without waiting for a reply, Elizabeth and Hank walked away, leaving Gillian without a choice.

Before she had a chance to change her mind and dash off after Elizabeth, Seth was by her side. "You ready?" he asked, as he folded the chairs and then tucked them under his arm. "I'll get these to Liz on Monday."

She wasn't ready, suddenly, but she followed him to his truck anyway, wondering how in the world she was going to handle things between them. What if he tried to kiss her again? What if he asked her for a date? How could she keep her heart safe from a man as wonderful as Seth Connor?

Chapter Five

"You're beat aren't you?" Seth observed as he opened the passenger door for her. "You need to give yourself a break and take tomorrow off."

Gillian was touched that he'd noticed her fatigue, and mentally compared him to some of the men she'd dated. Against Seth, the others fell short. They'd been friendly; he was charming. They'd been superficially casual; he was caring. She thought of how he'd been working late down at the hardware store and added responsible to the list. Quite a catch, if a girl were looking. Which she wasn't.

As he turned the engine over, then pulled the truck out onto the road, she tried for some light conversation. "You were right about the harmonica, but you forgot to tell me about the rest. You guys were wonderful."

"I'm usually right," he said with a grin. "You should have trusted me."

Okay, so humble wasn't on his list of good qualities. She figured he was kidding, but rose to the bait anyway. "You weren't right about Elizabeth. She was very nice and didn't pry for any information at all."

"That's because I threatened to make her life miserable

if she did. You can believe what you want, but you'll find out the hard way if you trust her with your secrets."

She was afraid he might be right again, but she wasn't about to tell him so. "Time will tell, but I thought she was very nice," Gillian said. "I met your Aunt Maude too. Why didn't you tell me we're neighbors?"

Seth groaned. "You don't want to mess around with Aunt Maude either. Ever since Uncle Jerry died, she's been driving everyone crazy. When it comes to gossip and interference, she's even worse than Elizabeth."

"That's what Elizabeth said, but I think it's very nice that she cares so much. In fact, she's offered to help me get the shop opened up for business. Isn't that great?"

Seth turned and stared at Gillian for so long, she was afraid he was going to run the truck off the road. "She what?"

"She's going to help me out in the shop so I can get opened up for business. What's wrong with that?"

"You can't let her into your shop, Gillian, or you'll never get her out. She'll hang onto you like a bad habit and you'll never be able to break her once she gets ahold of you. I'm right about this."

Gillian was on the defensive in an instant, pushing his list of good qualities to the back of her mind. "How terrible to say something so mean about someone who's just trying to help. And she's your aunt, Seth. You should appreciate your relatives, but all I've heard you do is talk badly about Elizabeth and now your aunt too." She crossed her arms over her stomach and looked out the window at the inky blackness. "I can't begin to imagine how you must talk about your mother."

Seth was so quiet for so long that she finally snuck a peek in his direction. It was dark in the cab, but there was just enough light shining from the instrument panel for her to see that his jaw was stiff. That last remark had been below the belt.

"Look, I'm sorry. It's just that I never had extended family to love, you know? My mom and Joe were all I had. That's part of the reason I came back here. If I can't have real family of my own, I'll settle for friends and neighbors to care about, and maybe a stepmother too. It hurts to hear you talking negatively about your family, when I don't have any at all."

"Do you think I don't care, Gillian? Is that why I came home to take over the business when my dad had his heart attack and then stayed on after he died? Because I don't care?" He laughed, bitterly, and Gillian felt his pain. "I've put everyone else in front of myself and my dreams for nearly a decade, and you think it's because I don't care? Everyone needed something from me. Mother, Aunt Maude, Jackson, Elizabeth." He looked over at Gillian and she could see the stark pain in his eyes in the glare of headlights of an oncoming car. "I don't have anything left to give them anymore, Gillian. They've bled me dry. I've got to start living my life, following my own dreams, or I'm going to die. You, of all people, should understand that."

"What are your dreams, Seth?"

"I'm leaving for Charlotte at the end of the summer. Charlie Mahoney and I have a construction business that's just getting off the ground, and I need to be there."

She closed her eyes against the sudden sting of tears. Seth was leaving Ruby Valley? Charlotte was a place, not a person. Charlotte, North Carolina. She was jealous, just the same.

"I'm sorry I didn't tell you sooner, but it just never came up."

She shrugged. "There's no reason you should have told me. You don't answer to me in any way other than as someone I've hired to fix up my shop. Anyway, you're right. I do understand what it means to live with a dream in your heart. That's all that kept me going for years. It's why I'm here."

Seth reached across the seat and took her hand in his. He squeezed tightly for a minute before letting go. "I couldn't understand why you'd want to come back to a place that I'm so ready to leave, but I'm glad you did. It was the right thing for you to do, but it's not right for me. You've had a chance to get away and see what's out there in the world. Now it's my turn."

She nodded, suddenly more tired than she could bear, and they rode on in silence for the rest of the trip home. At her place, he pulled up to her cottage behind the shop and cut the engine, then turned to her.

"There's something you should know, Gillian, if Elizabeth didn't already tell you tonight."

She shook her head and reached for the door handle, not wanting to hear anything more just now. She had enough to think about for the time being and needed to be alone to deal with it.

Seth took her hand before she could slide out of the truck, though, and held her in place. "You have two little sisters named Heather and Kaylee. Patty, your father's widow, still lives in your old place, and she's waiting for you to call her. She wants you to call. I promised I wouldn't push you, but I think you really need to go see them, Gillian. It's time to get over the past and move on."

Her heart felt like it would pound right out of her chest, and she snatched her hand away in confusion. "What?" She was incredulous. "Why didn't you tell me this before?"

"I figured you needed to hear it from Patty, not me. I don't want to get in the middle of things between you two." He tried to take her hand again, but she pulled it from his grasp. She did *not* want to be touched at the moment.

"You didn't think it was important to tell me about two little girls who are my *sisters,* but it was okay for you to call Patty and talk to her about *me*? Isn't that what you did?"

"I didn't want her to hear about you from some stranger, that's all. There're the girls to think of, and you too. I just wanted to make sure no one gets hurt."

"Are you like the mayor of the neighborhood, or something? Everybody's hero? I've got news for you. I don't need for you to be my protector. I'm all grown up, just like your family, and I don't need your help any more than they do. And Patricia Guy and her daughters aren't even your family—they're mine! You involved yourself where you don't belong. Maybe you should take a good look in the mirror before you go pointing fingers at others."

Gillian got out of the truck and slammed the door, then ran to her house, unlocked the door, and slammed that behind her as well. She was trembling with anger and wanted so very badly to blame Seth since he was near and available, but she couldn't. He'd only told her the truth. The responsibility of telling her should have been her mother's. *She* should be the one feeling the brunt of Gillian's anger. How could she have kept something so important from her?

She tossed her handbag onto the couch and went straight to the kitchen phone. Her hand shook as she punched in her mother's number and listened to the first ring, then the second. Before the third, she hung up. What would it accomplish to confront Anita Guy in her present state of mind? Anita would just hang up and refuse to talk to her until she'd calmed down enough to be civil. Then, she'd twist the truth and find some way to blame someone else, most likely Gillian. That was just the way she was.

Gillian closed her eyes and rested her forehead on the wall next to the phone. She was so confused her head hurt. She had sisters she never knew existed, and Seth would soon be leaving. Both pieces of news had thrown her. They'd struck as quickly as diamondback rattlers, and she hadn't been prepared for either of them. It was as if a twister had taken her emotions and twirled them up inside her.

She wasn't sure what she was feeling about Seth leaving the valley. They'd only just gotten reacquainted, but there was the oddest sensation of loss tugging at her heart. And, while she was elated to find out she had sisters, she was also apprehensive about meeting them. What if they didn't know about her or didn't want to meet her?

She was confused and emotionally exhausted. Knowing it was futile to try to sleep, she changed into some grubby jeans and an old T-shirt, grabbed a flashlight, and headed across the dark lawn to the shop. Whenever she was angry or upset, she'd found it best to work it out physically. This way, she could kill two birds with one stone by working out her frustrations refinishing some old furniture. With the way she was feeling, she'd have the entire houseful of furniture refinished by morning.

Seth followed the familiar twisting highway up to his cabin in the foothills, trying unsuccessfully to keep his mind on the road. Why had he blurted it out like that? Why hadn't he just stayed out of it and let her find out for herself? Because she'd been hurting and he couldn't stand it. She needed someone to love, someone to make her feel like she belonged. Just for a minute, he'd wanted it to be him, and that scared him.

He didn't want to care about her that way. It was one thing to look out for her and help her get settled in and opened for business, but it was another thing entirely to fall for her. That was out of the question.

Once he was in his cabin, he poured himself a soda and turned on the television, determined to get his mind off of her. Maybe he should call one of his old girlfriends and go out for a night on the town. He frowned. Most of his old girlfriends were married now. In fact, most of them married the next guy that had come along after him. He was affec-

tionately known around town as sort of a last hurrah, he
knew. He was the last fling before a girl settled down for
good, and he'd always been flattered by that. Now, it just
made him feel empty and alone.

There was something happening between them, even if
she was a little mad at him at the moment. She might deny
it if he asked, but she'd felt good in his arms tonight, and
he'd seen interest in her eyes every time he'd looked, and
that had been plenty. Maybe they could casually date, keep
it light. Then, he could leave at the end of the summer
without any unfinished business holding him back. His curiosity would be satisfied, and this attraction to her would
be a thing of the past.

Then, she'd find some other guy to hook up with and
marry. They'd have a houseful of little redheaded kids, and
she'd run her little shop and become a beloved member of
the Ruby Valley community, just like she'd always
dreamed. He hated the very thought.

He closed his eyes and remembered how she'd felt in
his arms during their dance. He'd pulled her in just enough
to satisfy his curiosity, to see if they made a perfect fit.
They did. He hadn't expected to be so taken with her. But
he was.

So what was he going to do about it? They had the entire
summer to get to know one another better. Then what?
He'd leave, she'd stay, and that would be that. It didn't sit
well with him.

Sleepiness caught up with him and, slowly, his brain let
go of the questions that plagued him. He'd find no answers
tonight. With the vision of mossy green eyes haunting him,
he closed his own and went to sleep. He dreamed of a
redheaded tomboy running free through grassy fields.

Chapter Six

The letter fell from the bottom of the drawer as soon as she pulled it free of the oak dresser. It was in a yellowed envelope marked simply "John." There was no other marking on the envelope, and though it might have once been glued shut, it was no longer sealed. Gillian hesitated only a fraction of a second before slipping her finger between the flap and envelope and freeing the letter inside.

She felt a bit voyeuristic as she scanned the first few handwritten lines.

My Dearest John,

Today I watched you take Grace for your wife and my heart broke into a thousand pieces. Why did I ever let you go? My own ambitions blinded me to the fact that I now see as clearly as your beloved face in my mind: Love is everything. Without it, we are nothing.

As I watched you walk down the aisle today and claim her as your wife, I cried for the loss of our love and any chance of a life together. How will I live in her shadow and pretend I don't love you with all of my being? How will I stand by and watch her bear your children, knowing they could have been ours?

*Don't worry that I will cause you grief in your new
life. I'll keep our love to myself and cherish it always,
but please know that you'll be in my heart forever.*
                                            Yours always,
                                                      M.

Gillian let the tears fall unchecked down her cheeks. Her
heart went out to the woman who'd written the letter to her
John on his wedding day. How hurt she must have been,
yet she'd been at the wedding and wished him the best. If
she'd been in the woman's shoes, could she have done the
same?

She set the letter aside and pulled out the other drawers,
wondering if there'd been anything else with it. Who'd hidden it there? Or had it simply slipped back behind the
drawer and been forgotten over the years? A thorough
search of the dresser revealed nothing more and she felt a
touch of disappointment. She sat back and looked at the
old, battered dresser, wondering to whom it had belonged.
It was as old as dirt and had obviously been neglected in
recent years. It could have been sitting here in the basement
forever. The Keeneys had kept such shoddy records, she
doubted she'd ever know.

With a sigh, she folded the letter, slid it back into its
envelope, and tucked it into her jeans pocket. It was a
keeper and she wanted to place it in her box with the other
treasures she'd rescued over the years. Sometimes, she
could track down the owners, but she doubted this would
be one of those times.

She stood up and stretched her back, gauging the time
to be nearly 10 A.M. by the angle of the sun coming through
the basement window. She'd worked until nearly one in the
morning before she'd felt sleepy and calm enough to go to
bed, but had risen early, as was her habit, and had run off
the rest of her anger at Seth, if not her mother.

Reason had come with the light of day, and she knew

part of her anger was with herself for not getting in touch with Patricia Guy when she'd first come back to town. She should have, but she'd been a coward. Sometimes it was hard to remember she wasn't that dirty little tomboy she'd been all those years ago.

Carefully, she set the drawers off to the side where they wouldn't get accidentally kicked or tripped over, and climbed the rickety stairs to the kitchen, promising to return later and work a little more. She'd nearly forgotten how much she enjoyed the refinishing process of tearing the furniture apart piece by piece, cleaning and restoring each part, then putting it all back together again with loving care. It was satisfying to see the pieces come back together and know it would be loved and appreciated for years to come. If she could, she'd like to stay right where she was and work on a few more pieces, but at the moment, she had more important things to do.

After a shower and change of clothes, she had some family matters to attend to. There were two little girls out there who needed to meet their big sister.

An hour later, Gillian pulled her Rodeo off the highway onto the shoulder and shifted it into park, but she didn't cut the engine. Butterflies swarmed her insides. The certainty she'd felt about this visit suddenly faltered at the sight of her childhood home, and she wasn't precisely sure what she was doing there. It felt like a huge mistake to show up on their doorstep without warning, especially when that doorstep used to be her own.

She wallowed around in indecision for a moment, quickly considering alternatives. She could always go back home and simply call Patricia Guy and ask to meet her at some neutral location that wouldn't remind her so keenly of the past. She could almost hear her father's voice calling to her across the years.

But she was already here, sitting near the gravel drive.

She could just see the front corner of the carport through the trees, which had grown considerably, but that was all. If she put the car in drive and inched up just a smidgeon, she would be able to see the front yard and the front of the house too. Before she could chicken out, she tried it and shoved the gearshift into park again.

Her breath caught in her throat. It hadn't changed a bit. Even her willow tree was still there, though larger than she'd remembered. A movement beneath the tree caught her eye and she watched as a young girl, maybe ten or so, crawled out from beneath the branches and stared directly at her.

In terms of fight or flight, Gillian usually chose the former, but she suddenly felt the urge to drive away—and fast! Her hand hovered over the gearshift for a shaky moment, then pulled it down into gear. She eased the truck around into the drive, pulling all the way up to the house. With a bracing breath, she cut the engine and stepped out.

"Hi," she said to the scraggly redheaded girl, feeling completely transparent in front of her innocent eyes. "Is your mom at home?"

Without a word, the girl dashed across the yard and disappeared behind the front door of the house. A moment passed as Gillian wondered if she should follow, or if she should stay put in case the girl had actually gone to get her mother. Then, the door opened and a woman, much younger than Gillian had expected, stepped out onto the porch.

"You're here," she said simply.

"Patricia Guy?" Gillian had to force her voice out around the lump that had suddenly formed in her throat. She wiped her sweaty palms on her pants legs, then clasped her hands in front of her to keep them from shaking.

"Gillian," she said in a gentle, Southern-tinged voice. "We've been expecting you." She stepped off the porch and approached Gillian with open arms. Gillian could see she wasn't much older than herself, maybe thirty-four or thirty-five at the most. "I'm glad you decided to come by and meet us finally." She gathered Gillian close for a quick hug, then led her into the house.

"I guess you heard I'd moved back to town. I'm sorry I didn't call sooner, but I've been busy working on my shop and . . ." she let her words trail off. They sounded lame even to her. "I was afraid."

Patricia smiled warmly and hugged Gillian again, then pointed to the couch and said, "Have a seat and I'll get some iced tea and cookies. The girls and I baked them when we heard you might come by."

"How did you know?" she asked, then answered her own question. "Seth."

"Don't be mad. He handled things badly and wanted to try to set them straight again. Now, make yourself comfortable, and I'll be right back."

Gillian sat and looked around the living room while she awaited Patricia's return. She couldn't help but note the improvements that had been made over the years. The once bare wooden floors were now covered with an attractive rose-colored carpet. The walls were painted a soft cream with a floral print border. The furniture had been replaced and one whole wall that used to be bare was now covered in shelving that held a variety of knickknacks and trophies which she decided to investigate further.

The trophies were a surprise, something she might have expected in a houseful of boys rather than two young girls, but there they were with the girls' names boldly displayed. Gillian felt a surge of pride, and just a twinge of envy. She'd never had the opportunity to join organized sports and earn a trophy. She ran her finger over the graceful curves of a ballerina. Heather, it seemed, favored dance. A soccer player caught at the moment of impact between foot and ball graced one of Kaylee's trophies, and a ballplayer with bat poised to swing stood tall on another. The younger one favored sports like Gillian once had. She wondered if it was the ragamuffin she'd talked to outside. *Good for both of you,* Gillian thought, hoping she'd have the privilege of mentoring two growing girls. *Go out there and define yourselves as young women.*

Patricia came back into the room carrying a tray of tea and cookies and set them on the coffee table. If she was displeased with Gillian's explorations, she didn't show it. Instead, she sat down in an overstuffed chair and tucked her feet beneath her, looking relaxed and comfortable, while Gillian felt anything but.

"The girls and I decided that I should see you alone first, and then they'll come meet you when you're ready. Seth explained that you didn't know about them until yesterday."

Gillian was going to have to have a little talk with Seth later about butting in where he didn't belong. "I was never told about them. Maybe if my father had written, I could have visited before now and gotten to know them," she said, a trace of bitterness lacing her words.

"Your father did write you," Patricia said earnestly. "He sent you birthday cards and asked you to write him back. He would have paid for you to come visit if you'd have just responded to any one of his letters. We sent you pictures of the girls when they were born, and I tried to see you after the funeral, but your mother whisked you away so quickly that there wasn't the chance."

Gillian recognized the truth in her words and accepted them, though in doing so, she was accepting that her own mother had withheld the truth from her. It hurt, but it was just the sort of thing her mother would do. "My mother never said anything about my father after he remarried, and I never heard anything from him so I . . ." She shrugged helplessly, then finished lamely, "I didn't know." A sob rose up in Gillian's throat and she jumped up from the couch to pace the tiny room and get control of her emotions. "My mother was bitter even after she met Joe and remarried. I think she only told me about Daddy's marriage to you so I'd quit wanting to see him again. I'm surprised she brought me back for his funeral, to tell you the truth. We stayed over in Sylva and drove to the cemetery for the graveside service, then we left and went back home."

"He loved you. He'd have wanted you to know that." Patricia's eyes were warm and sincere, and Gillian knew she'd found a friend. "I wish the girls could have known him. They'll be interested to hear what kind of daddy he was since they can't remember him, except through pictures."

Gillian smiled through her tears. "I'd love to share him with them. How long have they known about me?"

"I'm not the kind of mother who keeps things from her daughters. I wanted them to know the truth, as difficult as it may be, so they'll be strong when they grow up. They've known about you since they were old enough to understand. Would you like to meet them now?"

Butterflies took flight in her stomach as she nodded. "Yes, but tell me about them first."

"Heather is twelve, and Kaylee is eleven. They're exactly twelve months apart and folks think they're twins since they share a birthday, but they're as different as night and day. I used to show them pictures of you from when you were a little girl; it's amazing how much Kaylee looks like you when you were her age. I can see she'll grow up to be a beautiful woman."

Gillian blushed at the compliment and fluttered a hand in the air in a manner completely foreign to her, then tucked it safely into a pocket once she realized what she was doing. "I have some things for them in the car, so I'll just run out and get them, if that's okay. Tell them I'll just be a minute." Gillian dashed outside and grabbed the boxes she'd put together and stashed in the back of the Rodeo earlier that morning. She'd gotten the idea while she'd been working on the furniture during the night.

"What's all this?" Patricia's lighthearted laughter greeted her when she walked back into the house. "You'll spoil them, if all that's for the girls."

"It's not much, really, I just wanted to give them something special."

"Well, I'm sure they'll appreciate it. They don't have grandparents living anymore to spoil them and their only cousins live in Seattle, Washington, of all places, so the only presents they get are at birthdays and Christmas."

Gillian nodded her understanding. It had always been the same for her. "You don't have anyone else?"

Patricia gave Gillian's shoulder a quick squeeze. "We have you," she said, then excused herself to get her daughters.

A moment later, she returned. "Gillian?" Patricia stood in the doorway, a blond-headed beauty tucked beneath her arm and plastered against her side. "I'd like you to meet Heather. Heather, this is your sister Gillian."

Gillian took a tentative step forward, then was propelled backwards as Heather launched herself into Gillian's arms and held on for dear life. If Gillian had held out any hope of getting through this meeting dry-eyed, they were dashed in that instant. Tears ran freely down her face, down Patricia's face, and from the moistness she was feeling through her shirt, down Heather's face as well. But, tears soon turned to laughter and they hugged each other until they couldn't stand up anymore, then collapsed on the couch to hug some more.

"I'm so pleased to meet you, Heather," Gillian finally managed, as she wiped the tears from her eyes. "I've always wanted a sister."

"I have an extra one you can have," Heather replied with a twinkle in her very moist eyes.

"Heather," Patricia admonished. "Don't mind her, Gillian, she and Kaylee would sell each other on the street corner if I let them. It's because they're so close in age."

Gillian just laughed. How wonderful to hear family talk this way, she mused. Then she thought of how Seth talked about his cousins and aunt. Was this the same thing, then? She'd missed so much growing up an only child. "Speaking of your sister, where is she?"

Heather looked at her mom, seeking permission perhaps, before she answered. "She's not so sure about meeting you, so she's sort of hiding."

"That's okay. If she needs some time to get used to the idea, I understand."

"So, do we get to see what's in the boxes, or do we have to wait until Kaylee shows up?"

"Heather!" Patricia directed a stern look at her daughter. "Mind your manners."

"It's alright, really," Gillian assured Patricia before turning to Heather. "Do you want to have a look? Kaylee can see later on when she's ready."

"Yes. I'll bet if she knew you were bringing presents, she wouldn't have run off. It serves her right."

Gillian reached into the first box and pulled out the first package, then handed it over to Heather. "Don't be too hard on her. It's hard to adjust to change." She sat back and watched as Heather opened the gift, hoping she'd like it, fearing she wouldn't.

"Oh, Mom, come look at this," cried Heather, as she dangled a delicate silver locket from its fragile chain. "It's beautiful, Gillian, thank you."

Gillian was thrilled she liked it. Leaning closer, she showed Heather how to open the clasp to display two tiny photos, one of Gillian and one of their father. "You can replace the photos, if you'd like, but I wanted to give you something personal. Now, here, let me put it on you, and then you can open the next one."

Heather lifted her blond hair off her neck so Gillian

could manage the clasp, then fingered the locket while Gillian dug for her next present. "I'll keep these pictures."

"Here. Open this one." She handed over a package a little larger than the one before it.

Eagerly, Heather ripped it open to display a beautiful silver antique jewelry box.

"You've got to have a place to store your locket when you're not wearing it, and I thought this would be just the thing. If you turn this key, it plays a tune, see?" Delicate tinkling notes came from the box, gaining Gillian another hug from Heather.

"Now, the last present is for both you and Kaylee, so I think she should be here to help open it." Gillian looked to Patricia. "Do you think it would be okay for me to go and find her?"

"I'm afraid she's down at the river, and it's quite a ways from here, I'm sure you'll recall. Maybe you can save it for next time you come. When she gets like this, there's no telling how long she'll stay down there."

So the one that looks like me, acts like me. Isn't that interesting? "I think I know the way, if you don't mind me trying to find her."

"You have to go through Mr. Mackey's cow pasture, Gillian. That's gross," Heather protested, wrinkling her nose.

"I've done it a time or two, so I think I'll survive."

"I'll have a towel and washcloth waiting for you when you get back so you can wash up," promised Patricia. "And if you're not back in an hour, I'm calling 911."

Gillian laughed and waved as she let herself out the back door. If Kaylee was hiding where Gillian thought she was, they'd be back long before that.

Grateful she'd dressed in her comfortable Nikes and shorts, she gingerly climbed the barbed-wire fence that separated their property from Mr. Mackey's. She smiled when she encountered the cows, and remembered how she used to call them names to scare them away, sure they'd give chase at any moment. The grass wasn't as tall as she remembered, and the walk not as long, but the path they'd beaten down as children was still there for her to follow. So much was the same, yet so much had changed.

When she reached the oak, she almost didn't recognize it. It was much larger than she remembered, and for a moment, she was sure no eleven-year-old could have climbed its lofty branches. But then she heard the leaves rustle above her head and knew she'd been right on target.

"If I look up, you're not going to drop a rock on my head, are you?"

"That's stupid. Why would I have a rock up a tree?" It was clear Kaylee didn't have the same blood lust that Seth and Charlie had had.

"No reason. Just asking." Gillian rubbed her scar and dared a glance up. No rock, just Kaylee. She took that as a good sign. "I have some presents for you back at the house. Don't you want to come back with me and open them up?"

"No. Why should I?"

"Ouch. You know you don't only look like me, you sound a bit like me too. That's definitely something I would have said when I was your age."

When Kaylee didn't respond, Gillian frantically searched for some way to connect with the girl. "I'll bet those were your soccer trophies on the shelf in the living room, weren't they? I never got to play soccer, but I always thought it looked like fun."

"You probably did girl things like Heather." It was almost an accusation.

"Sometimes I do now, but when I was your age, I was a tomboy."

Kaylee wasn't buying it. "You were not. You're just saying that to get me to come down."

"Okay, I'll prove it. I'll bet I can skip a rock clear across the river to the other side. No regular girl could do that, now could she?"

Kaylee giggled. "Heather sure can't do it. I can get it almost all the way, though."

"If you'll come down here, I'll prove I can." Gillian hoped the offer would be too good to pass up, but Kaylee didn't seem to be biting at the bait.

"Kaylee?"

Gillian got a whimper for an answer.

"What's wrong?" she asked, trying to keep the concern from her voice.

"My foot's stuck, and I can't get it out." Kaylee's whimper turned into a full wail, nearly making Gillian's hair stand on end.

What in the world should she do? It was a fifteen-minute walk back to the house and another fifteen minutes back to the river. And who was going to climb the tree to help Kaylee anyway? Patricia? Not likely.

She stood back and examined the tree, which now seemed three times larger than it had just a few minutes ago. Circling the base, she looked for a way up, but came up empty. How in the world had the kid climbed it in the first place?

"Kaylee? How the heck did you get up there anyway?"

Kaylee sniffled and tossed down a rope. "I used this."

"Of course you did."

Knowing there was no other way out of this predicament, she grabbed the rope and began her climb. When she was sure she'd never make it to even the lowest branch, she felt a helping hand on her arm pulling her up.

"You made it." Kaylee sounded as relieved as Gillian felt.

"And we'll see what good that does us, kiddo. Let's take a look at your foot."

She'd wedged it in between two branches and couldn't get the leverage to pull it free without falling out of the tree, but Gillian was able to slip her foot right out of her shoe, and then wiggle the shoe out of the branches. Kaylee was free and scrambling down the rope before Gillian could get her bearings.

"Hey, wait up, Kaylee. I may need you to rescue me if I fall down and break my neck."

"Just grab the rope and slide down. It's easy."

Had Gillian ever been that much of a tomboy? She doubted it, but since she could see no other means of escape, she took Kaylee's advice and grabbed the rope.

She landed on the soft bank on her rump with a good rope burn or two, but none the worse for wear. Somehow, she felt more exhilarated than she had in years. "I may have to do that again," she said, smiling. "But not today. We have rocks to skip."

Kaylee and Gillian scoured the riverbank for the flattest, smoothest river rocks they could find. When they had a small pile mounded up near the bank, Kaylee let one fly, nearly reaching the other side. Tucking a small rock into the curve of her index finger and thumb, Gillian pulled her arm back and flung the rock forward with such force, she was surprised she didn't throw her shoulder out of joint. To her delight, the rock skipped five times clear across to the other side of the river, just as she'd promised.

Kaylee stood in awe for about two seconds, then tried to beat her. Soon, all the rocks in their pile were gone and they stood facing each other. It was like looking into a mirror of the past.

"So, you ready to go open those presents?" Gillian draped an arm casually around Kaylee's shoulders, giving the girl room to pull away if she didn't want the contact.

"Are they girly things?" The contempt for all things *girl* was evident in her voice, as it had once been in Gillian's.

"Some of them are, but I'll tell you a secret that your sister doesn't know."

Kaylee's huge green eyes were glued to Gillian's. "I was

hoping one of you would be like I used to be, so I packed some sports-themed Beanie Babies and packs of old base-ball cards, just in case."

"You did? That's cool."

Gillian gave her a quick hug and then led the way back to the house. Along the way she discovered that Kaylee liked to fish as much as Gillian used to, and had actually won a prize in a trout fishing contest over in Bryson City last summer. Plus, Kaylee hated fried okra just as much as Gillian did.

When they arrived at the house, they were fast friends, much to the relief of Patricia, and they spent the rest of the afternoon happily chatting away and looking over the trin-kets and treasures that Gillian had given them. All too soon, it was time for her to go, but she left with a promise to visit again and an open invitation for them to come to her shop whenever they wanted, as long as it was okay with Patricia.

She waved one last time as she pulled out of the drive and turned toward home. She was fairly bursting with hap-piness and found herself singing some of the tunes Seth and Jackson had played the night before. She couldn't find it in herself to be put out with Seth, even though he'd put his big nose in her business, because everything he'd said had been true. She had a family to love, and it was rather sweet of him to want to make it easier for her to get to know them.

Of course, it wouldn't have been necessary if her mother had just been honest with her all those years ago and had told her about the girls in the first place. No wonder she'd been dead set against Gillian moving back to the valley. She'd known that all the little secrets would be uncovered and Gillian would learn the truth. Well, she had. Perhaps later, after she'd worked a bit longer on the furniture, she'd give her mother a little call.

Chapter Seven

Her morning run was getting off to a soggy start with the onset of unexpected rain, and she almost wished she'd slept in, but after her phone call with her mother last night, she needed to run off some leftover emotions. With each squishy splat of her running shoes against the pavement, she tried to leave a piece of her anger behind, but it wasn't easy. Her mother had spent years lying to her, withholding the truth because she'd been afraid to lose Gillian's love. More likely, she'd wanted to withhold Gillian's love from her father to hurt him. It was unforgivable. Unfortunately, there wasn't anything she could do about it now except make it up to her sisters.

The thought of Heather and Kaylee lifted her spirits a bit. *What a gift they are,* she marveled, pleased that they'd been so eager to forge a sisterly bond. Had she ever been that easy as a child?

She'd always wanted sisters. Patricia had promised they could visit as often as they'd like, and Gillian hoped they'd even come to spend the night occasionally. They could pitch a tent and camp beneath the stars or roll out sleeping bags on her living room rug and have a slumber party. They'd probably like that. So would she.

The sound of an approaching car pulled her out of her thoughts and, though she moved further onto the shoulder as she heard its approach, she still managed to get a good spray of gritty mud on her face and clothes. She'd only run about a mile of her usual three-mile route, but it was dangerous to be on the roadside. Even as she thought it, a truck approached from behind, passed her with a honk of the horn and another generous spray of mud, then pulled to the side of the road in front of her.

It was *Seth*. Her heart did a little somersault.

The passenger door opened and Seth's head appeared. "Need a lift?"

Gillian jogged up to the truck and hopped in, soaking the seat and Seth too as she flicked water and mud from her arms and face like a wet sheepdog. "Sorry," she said, feeling anything but. He'd sprayed her first, after all.

"No problem." He tossed her a towel from behind the seat and pulled the truck back out onto the road. "Bad day to be out running."

"Started after I left," she explained, shivering a little. She rubbed her arms and legs as dry as possible, then glanced at her waterlogged watch and noted the time. "It's just after seven. What are you doing up and out so early?"

"I need to get some supplies from the store, but it's too wet to haul the plywood in the pickup. I'll do some odd jobs around the place until it clears."

"I'll put on some coffee then, just as soon as I shower and change."

"Sounds good," he said, as he pulled the truck into the antique shop's drive and delivered Gillian all the way back to her cottage door. "I'll wait for you here while you get cleaned up."

"No, you go on. I'll be up in a few minutes." She was touched that he'd offered to wait. She opened the door and dashed into the cottage.

As quickly as she could, she drank down a bottle of water, showered, changed into jeans and a T-shirt, and pulled her hair back into a wet ponytail. Then she grabbed a couple of travel mugs from her kitchen cabinet, poured some of the coffee she'd brewed earlier, and found an old newspaper to hold over her head for the walk up to the shop.

When she let herself out the door, she was surprised to see Seth still waiting for her in the truck. She'd taken at least fifteen minutes or so getting cleaned up. He really was such a sweetie. She felt a tug on her heart.

"Thanks for waiting," she said when she was settled back inside the truck. "I brought you some coffee."

He folded the newspaper he'd been reading, tucked it back behind the seat, took the mug from her for a ginger sip, then handed it back to her so he could shift the truck into reverse. "I meant to tell you the other day that you need something done with the cottage porch railing and steps," he said. "You're going to put your foot through a step one day, those boards are so rotten."

"You can do it after the shop's open and I have a positive cash flow. That's my first priority."

Seth shook his head. "Safety should be the first priority. I'll take a closer look at it when the rain clears."

Gillian bristled at his authoritative tone. He was a sweetie, but she was still in charge here. "Thanks, but I really can't afford more than we've already agreed on. I'll be careful. You don't have the time right now, anyway."

Seth pulled the truck around to the front of the shop and parked as close to the shop's front door as possible, then cut the engine. "I'll put in extra hours to get it done so that's not an issue. If money is, we'll barter, because I'm not going to put it off and have you get hurt."

Barter? Gillian was intrigued. "What did you have in mind?" she asked, thinking of some of the interesting tools she'd unearthed down in the basement the other day. He might be interested in some of them.

He turned sideways in his seat and draped an arm across the back so his hand was behind her shoulders. "Well, let's see," he said, as he toyed with her ponytail, causing delicious little shivers to run down her spine. "How about dinner? You cook?"

"Only if you want me to burn the place down," she said with a shake of her head. "I don't cook." It was true. She could manage exactly three appliances in a kitchen, and the stove wasn't one of them.

"We'll go out then," he said, moving his hand from her ponytail to her neck where he traced tiny little circles that duplicated themselves in her stomach.

"I don't think that's such a good idea," she said, shifting the coffee mugs to one hand, then pulling at the door handle with the other. The truck cab was suddenly way too small for both of them. She needed to put some distance between them to try to regain some perspective. Just the thought of having dinner with him did all sorts of woozy things to her stomach.

Seth grinned devilishly, as though he knew exactly what she was feeling. "You're not afraid to share a little meal, are you?"

Bull's-eye. He made a direct hit, and she knew he knew it. She never backed down from a challenge. "It's a deal."

"I'll get started on the steps tonight."

Which would mean he'd be camped on her doorstep tonight, so they might as well share a meal after all. She wondered how he felt about Lean Cuisine. "Alright, dinner, but I warned you—I don't cook."

His warm eyes sparkled with victory. "Doesn't matter."

"We'll see if you still feel that way after you've eaten," she said, then handed him his mug and was out of the truck and up the stairs before he could respond. She unlocked the door and went inside, figuring he'd follow when he was ready, hoping the rain would pick up just a tad when he did. That man needed a good soaking.

A couple of hours and some odd jobs later, Seth stopped working long enough to stretch and listen to Gillian humming a song he'd played at the square, noting with a smile that she couldn't carry a tune. He'd had a great time playing with Jackson that night, the best time he could remember having at the Square. He'd been playing for her.

When he'd awakened Sunday morning, she'd been the first thing on his mind. He hadn't liked that one bit, but there it was. It didn't matter that he didn't want to be attracted to her or that he was totally baffled by how quickly it had happened. He just was.

Maybe it had to do with their past. They'd always shared a bond. When his father had become too much for Seth to take and Gillian's mother had ignored her one time too many, they'd been there for each other. He wanted to be there for her now.

To that end, he'd made a decision. He was going to be a friend to her and nothing more. A fling between them couldn't possibly come to any good. If he was going to move so far away that they'd never see one another again, that might be one thing. One last great affair to remember, or something like that. But, that wouldn't be the case with them. They'd see each other each time he came back to visit at Christmas or Easter and that would be awkward for both of them. He didn't want that for her. The best thing to do was to ignore their feelings and pretend they were nothing more than friends. That way, he'd be able to leave with no regrets for either of them.

He wasn't sure where the idea of dinner had come from. It had just popped out of his mouth, and he'd been delighted when she'd accepted. He'd known she'd accept the challenge. It wouldn't be a problem for them to have one simple little dinner together though. Friends had dinners together all the time.

The jingle of the little bell Gillian had hung from the front door pulled Seth from his thoughts, and he listened as Aunt Maude made her arrival on the scene. He wondered why she'd volunteered to help Gillian. Was she going to try to control her the way she tried to control his family? He shook his head. Poor Gillian. She didn't stand a chance against his meddling aunt.

Under the guise of forgetting a tool downstairs, he went down and listened in on their conversation.

"I'm glad you'll be helping me with the place," Gillian was saying. "There's so much to be done."

Aunt Maude smiled. "I can't do any heavy lifting, but I'd be happy to help you clean the clutter."

"Would you? Everything downstairs has been dusted and I'm working on taking inventory, but the upstairs hasn't been touched yet. Seth's creating quite a bit of dust up there, so there's no point in trying to clean yet, but it would be nice to bring some of the better pieces down here to display them. Do you think you could go up there and choose some small pieces?"

Maude beamed. "I'd be happy to." Seth nearly choked.

He stepped to the side as Gillian took Maude on the grand tour, and followed as they moved upstairs. He'd never seen Maude so agreeable and was suspicious about her motives. What was she up to?

As soon as Gillian went back downstairs, leaving Maude upstairs to look around, Seth followed and cornered her. "She's up to something."

Gillian rolled her eyes. "Really, Seth. She's your aunt. Be nice."

He followed her to her office and leaned against the doorway, watching as she settled into her chair and turned to the computer. She was bright, but gullible if she believed his aunt was just there to help. "Just watch her."

"Seth." Gillian turned her chair to face him and leaned back, crossing her arms over her stomach. "What's she going to do? Rob me blind? She lives next door, for heaven's sake."

How could he explain his gut instinct? Gillian wouldn't understand if he tried. "No, she'd never do that, but she's up to something; I just don't know what."

Gillian rose and pushed him out of the doorway, obviously turning a deaf ear to his warning. "Go back to work. I'll let you know if I need any more unsolicited advice, okay?"

"Don't say I didn't warn you," he said, waggling a finger at her, but did as she commanded and returned to work upstairs. It was a good thing he was going to be around while Aunt Maude was in the place. He could keep an eye on her.

A few hours later, footsteps on the stairs above drew Gillian's attention away from her computer screen. From the sound of things, it was Seth who was descending the stairs rather than his diminutive aunt. She wished she could understand Seth's untrusting opinion of the woman, but she had seemed the epitome of kindness and charity. Why was he so suspicious of her motives?

She looked up just as Seth popped his head into her tiny office. "It's lunchtime, and you've been in your hole all morning. Why don't we go over to the diner and grab a bite to eat?"

Her heart tripped and stumbled, but caution prevailed. She shook her head and turned back to the computer screen. "I've got too much to do, but thanks for the offer."

"Look, Maude just went home to get her own lunch, and the rain's finally stopped. We won't be gone for more than an hour, tops."

She shook her head without even glancing his way. They were already spending way too much time together.

"You need to eat and you need to get out of this place

for awhile. Now come on," he coaxed, pulling her gently but firmly out of the chair.

"I've been out," she protested, pulling her arm from his grasp, trying to ignore the tingling sensation his touch set off. She was suddenly feeling claustrophobic in her tiny office, especially with his six-foot frame filling every spare inch of airspace available. "I spent Saturday night and all day Sunday out too. I've got work to do."

Seth heaved a belabored sigh and reached for her again. "Are you always this difficult?"

Gillian batted his hand away, annoyed at his persistence, irritated by her heart's response to his touch. "Quit man-handling me. If you feel you have a point to make, kindly make it with words." How could she keep her distance if he kept invading her personal space?

Seth folded his arms across his chest and retreated a couple of steps to lean casually against the doorframe, his head cocked at an angle, as though contemplating his next move. After a long moment, he switched tactics and dangled a carrot she just couldn't refuse. "I have a surprise for you, but you aren't going to know what it is unless you come with me."

A surprise? Curiosity was a traitorous thing. She had work to do; she didn't have time for guessing games. "What kind of surprise?" she asked dubiously, interested in spite of herself.

He grinned his charming little lopsided grin and was transformed into the boy she once knew, convincing her to walk a fallen tree trunk across a creek bed or swing from a rope high above the river. At that moment, he was simply irresistible. "My lips are sealed."

That was no answer, but she could tell he wasn't going to spill it. An hour of time wasn't all that much. "Let me grab my purse from the cottage," she said, but as soon as she was on her feet, he firmly grasped her hand and led her out the front door, locking it behind them with his copy of her key. Then, he all but tossed her into his truck and shut the door firmly, as though afraid she'd change her mind.

"My treat," he said as he climbed in his side, then started the engine. "You don't need to bring a thing other than your beautiful self."

She laughed and blushed at the compliment, all the while warning herself to be wary of him. He was too charming for his own good . . . and hers too! "I'd better warn you, I eat like a horse."

"I haven't seen you eat more than a bird would, but I think I can handle it. My current client pays generously."

She slid a sidelong glance in his direction. "We can discuss a reduction in fees if I'm over-paying you. And don't be so sure you can afford my appetite. Don't you remember how much I used to eat at the church picnics? I have a deep-rooted love for cold fried chicken and potato salad."

He nodded. "Uh huh, I remember. Deviled eggs too. You stuffed them into your mouth until your cheeks bulged out and you nearly exploded."

"Oh, yeah, I'd forgotten about that." She smiled and felt her heart go all warm and fuzzy. He remembered.

They fell into comfortable silence and Gillian turned to gaze out the window. The sun shone brightly across a valley washed clean by morning rain. Wildflowers danced haphazardly across rolling fields, tiger lilies waved as they passed. The ever-present mountains rose nearby and hugged the land in a warm embrace. This was the valley of her childhood, the place of her dreams. This was home.

The Ruby Valley Diner was a favorite hangout of locals and tourists alike. Established in the late 1800s to feed the hungry ruby miners and their families, it had managed to survive two world wars and the Great Depression because it offered good food at reasonable prices with efficient, friendly service. Both Gillian's and Seth's families had eaten many Saturday night dinners there before attending Fiddlin' on the Square, and Seth thought it would be the perfect place to hold the reunion he'd orchestrated.

Suzie Maitland, luncheon waitress and Seth's youngest cousin on his mother's side, waved Seth and Gillian on back to a table. She was over in two shakes to pour ice water and slap down a couple of menus.

"Set two more places, Suz. We're expecting company." Seth smiled at his cousin and winked at Gillian's startled expression. "I'd like you to meet Gillian Guy, a former resident of the valley. Gillian, this is Suzie Maitland, my little cousin."

Suzie extended a hand to Gillian and nodded politely, then beat a hasty retreat to the kitchen without giving Gillian a chance to say hello.

Seth took note of her behavior and commented, "Either she's painfully shy, or she wants to be the first to spread the news that Gillian Guy has actually crawled out of her hole and is blessing the diner with her presence."

"Very funny. So, who else is coming?" she asked, looking a bit uneasy.

"It's time to renew some old acquaintances."

Gillian rubbed the tiny scar on her forehead in a gesture that was becoming familiar to Seth. He'd seen her do it when she was tired and frustrated and, now, nervous. "Which old acquaintances?"

"Just some old friends." He reached across the table to take her hand and soothe her apprehension, then chuckled when she yanked it from his grasp, a pretty stain of pink spreading across her cheeks. They were both in trouble, because he'd felt it too. "Why don't you go ahead and look over the menu since you're planning on eating enough for an army."

He picked up his own menu and pretended to study it, sneaking glances at her over the top as she turned nervous eyes toward the diner door. His heart beat hard against his ribs as he studied her delicate ivory skin and that wicked mane of fiery hair. Not the sophisticated beauty that spoke of money and breeding like you might find in a woman from one of the big cities like New York or Chicago, but an earthy strawberries-and-cream kind of loveliness that belonged exclusively to the rolling foothills of the Smokies. She was as radiant, vibrant, and delicate as the wild lilies that grew along the roadsides and just as tough too. It was both satisfying and painful to gaze at her. They didn't have very much time left together.

Now wasn't the time to entertain those thoughts, though. Today, he had other items on the agenda and one of them was helping her ease back into life in the valley. Saturday night had been a step in the right direction, but it wasn't enough. She'd been working herself so hard to get her shop opened up that she hadn't taken any time to get reacquainted with old friends. If she kept up this pace, she'd work herself into an early grave. Look what the place had done to the Keeneys, the old buzzards. He wasn't about to let the same thing happen to Gillian.

As though on cue, he looked up and saw his cousins, Jackson and Katie, making their way to the table. Though Katie was several years older, Seth remembered Gillian's fondness for his cousin and mentally crossed his fingers. He'd like to know she was among friends before he left at the end of the summer.

Katie, true to her amiable ways, didn't let him down. Her enthusiasm at seeing Gillian again was genuine and he had the satisfaction of seeing the uncertainty in Gillian's eyes give way to happiness as the older woman grabbed her shoulders and hauled her up for a great bear hug while Jackson slid into the booth next to Seth.

"Look at you! You're all grown up," Katie cried. "I guess I still thought of you as a little girl, and here you are a woman grown."

Gillian made a face. "You're not that much older than I am. What is it, eight years or so?"

"I may only be thirty-four, but my three boys make me feel like a senior citizen. I named all my gray hairs after them," she said, giving her Clairol-blond curls a shake.

Seth knew when a lady was begging for a compliment and didn't let her down. "There's not a gray hair on your head, and you know it, Katie."

Apparently, Gillian wasn't as concerned about the hair thing. She'd gotten stuck on the number of Katie's children. "Three boys? You've been busy!"

"Well, I married Billy Watkins," she said, as though that explained it all. At Gillian's blank look, she elaborated, "You were probably too young to know much about Billy, but at one time or another, he had most of the local girls in the backseat of his Charger. Sort of like Seth, here," she said, gesturing toward him and earning a chuckle out of Jackson. "I was the first one to refuse him, and he proposed within six months." She beamed with obvious pride.

"Well, good for you," Gillian said, all the while throwing darts at Seth with her eyes. Her disapproval did wonders for his ego, and told him more than she probably meant to. "How old are your boys?"

"Fifteen, fourteen, and twelve. Billy wanted to try for a girl, but I'm through. He may be approaching forty, but he's still as randy as a goat. I'm sure that's the way Seth's gonna be too. God bless the woman who finally lands him. Say, you're not married are you?"

Color stained Gillian's face at Katie's none-too-subtle hint and Seth considered strangling his cousin.

"I'm married to my business," Gillian said smoothly, then tactfully changed the subject. "I'd love to meet your family."

"You will, and all too soon I imagine. Billy is one of Ruby Valley's finest, but he spends most of his time chasing our kids around and keeping them out of trouble. We don't have much crime here, you know."

"We had too much in Florida with the tourists. The way they flash their money around makes them easy targets. I always had to be so careful when I traveled. It's one of the reasons I came back here."

Katie put her arm around Gillian's shoulders and gave her a quick squeeze. "I hope you came back to renew old friendships too."

Jackson, who'd been busy looking over the menu and giving Seth the lowdown on the morning's business at the hardware store, chose that moment to tune in to the conversation. "I'm not sure you want to get messed up with Katie's crew. Most of the town runs the other way when they see them coming." He yelped and grabbed his shin when Katie kicked him under the table.

Suzie returned to fill their water glasses again, leaning across Jackson to reach Seth's glass, which was as full as she'd filled it the first time since he hadn't even taken a drink. "You and Katie better behave yourselves in here, Jackson, or I'll have to make you leave. You wouldn't want that, now would you?"

Jackson gave her a grin and a wave as she went to the next booth. "I'll behave, Suz, I promise, but you know Katie here. She's a rowdy one."

"Hey!" Katie smacked Jackson over the head with a menu.

"Come on, you two," Seth reprimanded them. "Stop squabbling. Gillian doesn't appreciate family warfare."

Gillian laughed. "I don't mind. I'm beginning to realize it's how you express your love for each other."

"Squabbling is what we do best," said Katie. "Do you remember the fights that used to erupt at the Wednesday night church suppers when we were kids?"

Gillian wrinkled her brow. "I don't remember that, to tell you the truth."

"That's because you were usually off fishing with Seth. I don't know how you could stand to touch those nasty earthworms and crickets." She screwed her face up and shuddered. "I remember when I used to baby-sit you. You were such a quiet thing. Always had your nose in a book when you weren't running off into the woods."

"Well, I remember that you always had an ear glued to the phone and your eyes to the TV set. You never even knew I was gone when I'd slip out of the house."

"Of course I knew you were gone. Why do you think Seth showed up wherever you went?"

Seth could feel Gillian's eyes on him as he engaged Jackson in some inane conversation about hardware. Why had Katie brought that up?

"What do you mean?" Suspicion was ripe in her voice.

"Seth followed you so I didn't have to. It usually cost me a candy bar or soda, but it was well worth it so I didn't have to go tromping down through that nasty cow pasture to drag you back. He always delivered you home safe and sound and saved me the effort."

"Oh, really." Her eyes flashed.

He was in deep trouble. Those times with Gillian, fishing for trout in the Little Tennessee with cane poles and corn, watching for fireflies in the dying light, listening for the whine of the cicadas from the forest, had been special. It never occurred to her to question how Seth had always known when she'd be at the river, and he'd never enlightened her. Betrayal shone brightly in her eyes.

Before he could think of anything to say, Suzie returned with their orders. When she was gone, Jackson wisely changed the topic and brought the conversation around to safer ground. "How's your shop coming along? Think you'll be open by the fourth?"

Gillian toyed with her food, but didn't take a bite. "Should be open by the last week in June. I've still got rooms to wade through, but it won't take long, especially with Maude helping. Seth should have the repairs done by then too." She sent a meaningful glare his way. "Especially at the rate he's charging me."

Jackson let her comment pass and turned his eyes to Seth, surprised. "*Our* Aunt Maude is helping her?"

Seth raised both brows and nodded slowly, then shrugged. "You ought to see her in the role of humble servant. It's a sight."

"Why are you so surprised?" Gillian asked.

Neither cousin was immediately forthcoming, but Katie seemed to have no qualms about offering up a reason. "That Maude Strickland is a mean old bat and never did a thing for anybody but herself. What in the world did you offer her to help you?"

"Not a thing, actually. Ask Seth."

"It's true," he confirmed. "She's been helping and won't take a dime for it." He shrugged. "I wouldn't have believed it if I hadn't been there to see it for myself."

"Will wonders never cease? Old Maude Strickland doing a selfless act." Katie looked at Gillian with bewildered eyes. "You must have her under some kind of spell."

Seth watched Gillian duck her head, a blush stealing over her features, and knew he was under her spell too. There was just something about her that called to his protective instincts.

"I wish I could work magic spells. I'd have my place cleaned up and ready to go with the twitch of my nose."

"With Seth doing the repairs for you, you'll think you did." Jackson took a gulp of iced tea and asked, "What will you do for the Fourth? You gonna be ready for all those customers?"

"What happens on the Fourth?"

Jackson punched Seth in the arm, a familiar gesture between the two of them. "You didn't tell her about the Fourth? What's wrong with you?" Then he turned his attention back to Gillian. "It's a pretty big day for all of the local businesses. They have all-day specials with free refreshments. Folks sort of meander from store to store, starting downtown and working their way out to the fairgrounds for the carnival and fireworks. It's sort of an annual social and pilgrimage."

Gillian's eyes lit with excitement. "That sounds great. I could have coffee and cake or something. Do you really think folks would stop in? I'm all the way out on Highway Twenty-eight."

"If it's free, and you're on the way out to the fairgrounds. They've got to pass you to get there," said Katie, laughing. "You know, since you sell antiques, why not keep it simple and classic? How about tea and cookies? You don't even have to bake them yourself. My mom runs the bakery downtown and makes the most delicious tea cookies you've ever tasted."

Gillian sounded hesitant. "I'm not sure I can afford that right now."

Katie patted her hand. "Don't worry about that. I'll talk to her and see what she can do for you."

"Oh, I wouldn't want her to do anything special for me. If she's a businesswoman, she needs to make money too."

"Mom will cut you a deal; you're practically family. Isn't she, Seth?"

Seth glared at his cousin. Katie was matchmaking, and not very subtly either, unless she'd meant it in a "we're all one big happy family here in Ruby Valley" kind of way. He handled it the way all smart men handled a woman's loaded question—by avoiding a direct answer. "Katie's mom is everyone's mom, and I know she'd be hurt if you didn't let her give you a hand."

Gillian smiled. "If you're sure. I'll give you my card, and you can give me a call when you talk to her. I'll let you two decide on numbers since I have no idea how many customers to expect, but you've got to tell her I insist on paying her something, so don't go trying to get this done for free."

Katie took Gillian's card and tucked it into her purse. "Of course she'll charge you something. She wouldn't want to insult you."

Seth smiled smugly, pleased with himself for having changed the topic so smoothly. Later, he'd have to set the record straight for Katie. He and Gillian were going to be nothing more than friends. Good friends. "Now that that's settled, let's get to more important business, Gillie. How about going to the fair with me on the Fourth?"

"No fair. You beat me to it, Seth," complained Jackson. "I was going to ask her."

Seth shot his cousin an irritated look. *Jackson and Gillian? No way.* "You always were too slow."

"You always jump the gun."

"Down, boys! Both invitations are on the table and Gillian can consider them and then choose later. In the meantime, I've got to go see Mom about those cookies, and this girl," Katie put her arm around Gillian's shoulders and squeezed, "needs to get ready for a grand opening."

"Fine by me," Jackson agreed with a wink and a grin toward Gillian that had her blushing prettily and Seth ready to wring his neck.

Seth scowled at Jackson as he picked up the tab and tossed some bills on the table for Suzie. If Gillian were going to do any more blushing, he'd be sure Jackson wasn't the cause. She might be younger, but she had years on Jackson in maturity. Gillian needed someone older and more responsible to take care of her, not a kid like Jackson who didn't even know what he wanted in life.

Like me. He snuffed out the thought almost before it occurred. As attracted as he was to Gillian, he wasn't the man for her.

Chapter Eight

Seth's silence was a barrier that Gillian was anxious to breach as they followed the ribbon of highway back to her shop. She missed the easy camaraderie they'd shared on the ride to lunch earlier, even if she was still a bit stung by the fact that Katie had actually paid him to baby-sit her.

"Do you think the repairs will be finished by the Fourth?" she asked, trying for a lightheartedness she didn't feel. It was obvious that something was bothering him.

"I said the end of June. I meant the end of June."

His curt reply baffled her. "Is something wrong?" she asked, wondering what she'd missed back at the diner.

"Nothing's wrong," he said, keeping his eyes on the road ahead.

She crossed her arms and narrowed her gaze at him. "You sure have a strange way of showing it."

"I guess I was a little surprised to see you blushing over Jackson. Are you thinking about going to the carnival with him?"

Her first reaction was to laugh. "Jackson? He was just kidding around."

Seth raised his brows. "You sure about that? He seemed interested enough to me."

Seth sounded a bit jealous to Gillian. "It's obvious he has a thing going on with Suzie."

He shook his head. "No way, not Jackson and Suzie."

She shook her head. Hadn't he noticed the way Jackson's eyes had followed Suzie everywhere? He'd only asked her because he'd thought it would annoy Seth. And apparently it had, which surprised her. "Well, you just wait and see who he has on his arm when that carnival rolls around. Anyway, I'm not going with anyone. I have a business to run and no time to play."

"You can't work all the time, you know. You've got to get out and have some fun, get to know people."

"I don't agree. I'll meet plenty of people when they come out to the shop. Once the shop is established, I'll have time to join the local chamber of commerce and . . ."

"That's not what I'm talking about. You need a social life too. Go to the carnival with me, Gillie. Be my date."

Her heart beat hard against her ribs. Seth's date? It was tempting, but she shook her head. "I can't, Seth. I've got to stay focused."

Seth chuckled.

"What?" She couldn't imagine what he found funny about the situation.

"Me chasing you. You used to chase me around all over the valley, wanting to hang with my friends and me, remember? I guess what goes around really does come around."

Gillian didn't find that the least bit funny. "Believe me, if I'd known you'd been paid to spend time with me, I'd never have tried to keep up with you. I don't have to buy my friends."

"That was a long time ago, and it wasn't like that."

Gillian raised an eyebrow in disbelief. "Did Katie call you to find me and pay you in candy to do it?"

Seth sighed heavily.

It spoke volumes to Gillian. There was no way he could explain himself out of it, and he didn't try.

The silence was a living thing, sitting squarely between them. Her thoughts tumbled about like gemstones unearthed at a ruby mine. Seth had been her friend, and then wasn't. Now he was again, for the moment, but soon he'd be gone. She needed time to sort out her feelings about him, and right now her thoughts needed to be on her shop.

She looked out the window and tried to focus on the vibrancy of the tiger lilies, the delicacy of the Queen Anne's lace smattering the pastures along the winding road, but their beauty was lost on her today. Nothing looked as bright as it had on the drive into town.

Seth leaned across the seat and took her hand in his, tightening his hold when she would have pulled it from his grasp. "It was never like that." He spoke softly, hesitantly, as though trying to find the words to make her understand. "I was glad to spend time with you, Gillian, especially fishing at the river. I needed your friendship just like you needed mine. You weren't the only lonely kid around, you know."

Gillian turned away from the window and raised one brow dubiously.

He glanced her way, then moved his eyes back to the road. "Honestly. We were always friends. No one had to buy it, Gillian, it just was."

She tried to blink back the tears that were suddenly there. "Then why did you let Katie do that? I'll bet Charlie got a real kick out of that."

"Because I was a growing boy who loved chocolate, and I loved the fact that she was willing to pay me for something I'd have done for free. And Charlie never knew about it 'cause then I would've had to share my candy."

She felt a little catch in her heart. His words rang true, and she had to give him the benefit of the doubt, though she'd never forget his betrayal to their friendship when he'd clocked her with that rock.

As though he'd read her mind, Seth ventured an explanation. "I really didn't mean to hit you, you know. Charlie was going to bean you with it, so I tried to grab it from him. It was slick and just slipped out of my hands."

A single tear slipped free and slid down her cheek. Why did this man have the power to make her cry? She *never* cried. She freed her hand from his grasp and dashed the betraying tear from her face. "Really?" She hated the vulnerability she heard in her voice. It made her feel like a twelve-year-old all over again.

"Really."

When Seth laced his fingers through hers, she didn't pull away. "Why were you guys running away from me?"

"We were going skinny-dipping, and we didn't want you tagging along." He waited a beat, then added, "Although, looking back, I wish I hadn't been so afraid of you. Skinny-dipping could have been enlightening."

Once again, Seth managed to fluster her and knock her off balance. Her heart fluttered about in her chest like the gentle beat of butterfly wings, even as her arms closed protectively over her chest.

Seth's eyebrows wiggled suggestively. "I have to say, I like how things turned out."

"Keep your eyes on the road, Romeo."

His eyes swung back to the road ahead, but not before she caught the wicked twinkle dancing within them.

"Just saying it like it is, Sparky."

Gillian rolled her eyes at him and tried to get a handle on her runaway heartbeat. He was making her feel like a love-struck teenager. Is this how it would have been if she hadn't ever moved away? Or would they have been nothing more than friends? If he kept up his outrageous flirtation, how was she going to keep her heart from plopping right out at his feet?

As Gillian wrestled with her emotions, Seth turned the truck into the drive, slowed to a stop beside the shop, and cut the engine. He turned toward Gillian and reached over to toy with a lock of her auburn hair. "So, how about the Fourth? Will you go with me?"

Making a last-ditch effort to stay emotionally unattached from this man who touched her heart at every turn, she said, "I really do have too much work to do."

He gently pulled the curl he held captive. "Don't give me that. No one's going to be shopping for antiques on the night of the Fourth of July. They're going to be out with their friends and family celebrating and watching fireworks, just like you should be. Come with me, Gillie."

It was a dangerous thing being alone with him, but she had to do something to jump-start her heart. It had all but ceased beating while awaiting her answer.

"Alright, but it's not a date," she said, then completely lost her tenuous grip on her heart as he leaned close and placed the barest whisper of a kiss upon her cheek.

A rap on the window had them springing apart like teenagers necking at Lookout Point. "What are you two doing in there?"

Gillian pulled the door handle with a shaky hand and stepped down out of the truck. "You startled me, Aunt Maude."

"I don't know how you didn't see me when you drove in. I was sitting right there on the front porch waiting for you to get back."

Seth hopped out and skirted the ladies, leaving Gillian to offer explanations. He loped up the front steps and disappeared inside the shop.

Gillian decided avoidance was the wisest way to deal with Maude's nosiness. Seth had warned her about it, and while she appreciated the help Maude was giving her in her shop, she didn't particularly want her help in running her life. If she'd wanted that, she'd still be living near her mother.

"Sorry I kept you waiting. Seth took me for lunch in town."

"I might have gotten a few more things done around here if I could have gotten inside."

Gillian led the way up the steps to the door. "I didn't realize we'd be gone so long, actually. Seth surprised me with lunch with his cousins."

Maude gave a rather unladylike snort. "He did, did he?"

"It was a nice surprise."

Maude shrugged. "Sounds a bit high-handed to me, dear. Next thing you know, he'll be running your store like he does his cousins'. He has quite a way with people, you know, getting them to do things and making them think it was their own idea."

Gillian let them into the shop, listening for the sound of Seth's hammering to determine his location. Satisfied that he was upstairs and safely out of earshot she turned back to Maude, who had settled herself at the card table in the parlor to work on polishing some silver.

"Seth is running his cousins' store? I thought it belonged to all of them."

"Well, it did until they bought him out. That was nearly a year ago, but you'll notice he's still there telling everybody what to do. He was supposed to be gone long before now, but he keeps extending the deadline, hanging on to that place with both hands."

"He's leaving at the end of the summer."

Maude smirked. "So he's been saying, but he's not gone yet. I think he likes the power. He runs the family just like his daddy did before him, and they all just let him do it."

That was a surprise. Jackson seemed an amiable, but capable sort. And Elizabeth . . . well, that one could certainly stand on her own two feet.

"His cousins, his mother, his friends—he's always been

in charge." Maude's eyes lit up, and she leaned forward in her chair. "I could tell you a story or two about it, if you'd like to hear."

She didn't. It suddenly felt like an invasion of his privacy. Luckily, the phone rang, giving Gillian an excuse to avoid any more of Maude's gossip. Making her excuses, she went into her office to answer the phone, which turned out to be a wrong number. She then tried to focus on some handwritten notes she'd made on some of her glassware, but her mind kept drifting to Seth.

Was he leaving like he said, or was he going to stick around? Would it matter to her either way? If he stayed, would she consider pursuing a relationship with him? If he was going to leave, could she dare to let him get closer before he did?

He was attracted, she knew. Well, she thought she knew. There was always the possibility she was misreading the entire situation. She thought back to their dance and near kiss last Saturday. Then today he'd asked her to the Fourth of July celebration and kissed her in the truck. No, she wasn't misreading anything. He was interested. And so was she. But what should they do about it?

Snatching up her purse, she rifled through it looking for her ever elusive bottle of ibuprofen. She had a headache and needed to get a handle on it before she ended up in bed with an ice pack on her head. Finally, she snagged the bottle, poured a couple of white-coated tablets into her hand, and washed them down with some bottled water. Thoughts of Seth were just too confusing.

An hour later, she left her office in search of Maude, giving up on work altogether. Her head was throbbing in spite of the medication she'd taken, Seth's hammering sounding like a jackhammer on her brain, and she couldn't concentrate on the computer screen anymore. The only option left was to go lie down until it wore off.

"It's probably that stomach virus that's been going

around. Either that or the cooking down at the diner. All that grease can make a person green around the gills," Maude offered.

Gillian was feeling worse by the moment. "I don't think it was the food. I've just been pushing myself too hard trying to get the store opened."

"You go rest then, and I'll stay here awhile and finish up."

"Thank you. Seth will finish up around five and lock up. Just let him know when you leave for the day. And tell him to forget about the porch steps until another time."

"I'll tell him, dear," Maude said, patting her on the shoulder. "Listen, I can stay a bit later than usual, so why don't you just give me your key. That way I won't hold Seth up. He's probably got a date tonight."

Gillian's head was throbbing and getting worse by the moment, and just the thought of Seth hammering away on her front porch made fresh waves of nausea roll through her stomach.

She hadn't planned on giving a key to Maude, but she didn't have the energy to argue. She'd just get it back from her tomorrow after breakfast. Digging into her pocket, she found it and handed it over. "Thank you."

"The pleasure's all mine, dear," Maude replied as she gently patted the back of Gillian's hand. "You just call if you need anything later."

Gillian promised she would and quietly slipped out the kitchen door. Maybe she'd feel better after a little rest. If so, maybe she'd give Seth a call and see if he still wanted to get together. They could always order out.

She instantly regretted the thought of food and dashed toward the cottage, anxious to sleep it off.

Chapter Nine

Angry rumbling thunder awakened Gillian from a sound sleep. Disoriented, she glanced at her bedside clock, surprised to see it was well past midnight. Lightning, bright and fierce, illuminated her bedroom, followed closely by another violent boom of thunder. Dry-mouthed and fuzzy-brained, Gillian switched on the table lamp and stumbled down the hall to the kitchen for a bottled water.

Another crack of lightning flashed and the windows rattled with the thunder as Gillian opened the fridge. She squinted against the bright light, then groaned in dismay when the room was suddenly plunged into darkness, instantly blinding her. Feeling her way past the iced tea pitcher, she grasped a water bottle and quenched her thirst before gingerly making her way into the living room.

Did she have any candles? A flashlight? Her brain was too fuzzy to recall where she'd stashed such supplies, and she doubted she'd find anything useful in the dark, anyway. Thinking was too much of an effort, so she felt her way along the wall, intending to go back to bed.

Another flash of light came through the window causing Gillian to stop and tense, waiting for the thunder to follow. She'd always been a little afraid of storms, though she wouldn't admit it to a soul. After a moment, she realized the thunder hadn't come after all. Maybe the storm was moving farther away.

The next flash of lightning and crack of thunder had her holding onto her chest, trying to keep her heart from jumping out. This time, light flooded the entire room before it was plunged into darkness again. The heavens unleashed their burden, and a torrent of rain beat upon the roof and lashed at the windows.

Another flash of light momentarily illuminated the living room, then was gone, rooting Gillian to the spot. She tried to clear her fuzzy head and focus. Something wasn't right. Using the wall as a guide, she made her way to the front door. Oblivious to the rain, she opened the door and stepped out onto the tiny porch. Wind whipped at her hair and rain soaked the nightshirt she'd put on before she'd lain down earlier. Eyes sharp, mind clearing, she stood watching, waiting.

There. Up at the shop. A light flashed in one of the downstairs windows. What was going on? Without hesitation, she dashed out into the wicked night, crouching low against the stinging rain. Too late, she remembered her bare feet as her toes sank into the soft, wet grass and was grateful she didn't have to run across the gravel drive to reach the house. Thunder and lightning crashed around her just as she made it to the back porch and tried to open the door. It was locked tight. Too late, she remembered she'd given her keys to Maude.

What am I going to do?

She quickly examined her options. She could run across to Maude's and get her key back, but she didn't want to scare the woman to death knocking on her door at this time of night and without electricity. She could call the police, but what would she tell them? "Officer, I saw a light in the window and it might be a big, bad bogeyman." That'd be all over town by morning. Seth had the only other key, but she was reluctant to call him. She didn't want to be another of his dependents.

Another flash of lightning nearly made her hit the deck and she had to stifle a scream when the windowpanes rattled with the boom of thunder. Whether she liked it or not, the only option, it seemed, was to make the rounds around the house to check for signs of entry. If she only had a flashlight, it would be much easier; but then, if someone was inside, it was better for her to remain unseen. A flashlight would give her away.

Slowly, she crept across the yard and up the back steps, then peered inside the shop's kitchen window, making sure to stay as hidden as possible. Seeing nothing but darkness, she crept back down the stairs and worked her way around the side of the house. She tugged on each window that she could reach, checking to see if any were unlocked. The basement windows were the only ones she could reach and they were secure. The first-story windows were shut but too high off the ground for her to reach. If anyone had gone through those they'd have had to have a ladder.

Using her hands to shield her eyes from the pouring rain, she looked up at the second-floor windows, wishing she could see them better, but the darkness and lashing rain made it nearly impossible to see more than a few feet in front of her face.

Lightning flashed and the crack of thunder that followed quickly on its heels had her jumping yet again. She'd forgotten for a moment how much she hated storms, but it was quickly coming back to her.

Quickly, stealthily she climbed the front stairs, remaining low as she tiptoed across the slick porch, trying to maintain her balance. All she needed was to wipe out and end up on her backside. She peeked inside each of the four porch windows, but still couldn't make out anything inside because of the darkness of the night. Where was the lightning when she needed it?

Maybe I imagined it, she thought. It was probably just the light from a passing car shining through the house, or lightning reflecting off dresser mirrors in some sort of bizarre optical illusion.

Feeling a little foolish, she tried the front door, and finding it locked, dashed back down the porch steps and across the lawn to the cottage porch. She wiped the rain from her eyes and took a few calming breaths before she looked back up at the house.

It had to have been her imagination. Maybe a lingering effect of the headache or medicine. How could someone have gotten inside without breaking a window? Both outside doors were locked tight. Muttering at her own foolishness, she was about to go back inside to dry off, change, and go back to bed when a flicker of light from an upstairs window made her freeze in her tracks.

There it was again. Her heart pumped double-time as adrenaline flooded her body. It wasn't just her imagination! Someone was inside her shop!

Her instincts told her to find the source of the light, but practicality made her admit that wasn't an option without the key. So she was back to her earlier choices. Run through the rain to Maude's and risk giving the woman a heart attack, call the police, or call Seth.

As much as she hated to rely on Seth, she had to admit he was the least of the evils. She couldn't just bang on that poor old woman's door in the middle of a dark, stormy night. Besides, if she found an intruder, Seth would be of more help than an eighty-year-old woman. And she was loath to call the police and gain the reputation as a hysterical female.

After closing and locking the cottage door behind her, she worked her way through the pitch-dark living room, dripping water everywhere and stubbing her toe on the door as she reached the kitchen. She was still muttering under her breath as she located the wall-mounted phone and dialed information. After first talking to a recording, and finally, an actual person, she was connected. She rubbed her aching toe and sent up a prayer of thanks that the wall-mounted phone didn't require electricity.

A groggy-sounding Seth answered on the third ring. "What?" he barked, making Gillian wonder at the wisdom of calling him after all.

"It's Gillian," she said, startled by the sound of her own voice and suddenly sensing her vulnerability in the dark. She wished she'd stopped to get a butcher knife from the block on the counter before she'd made the call.

"Gillian? What's wrong?"

"I need the key to the shop," she whispered. "I think someone's inside."

Seth's voice was suddenly crystal clear, devoid of sleep. "Where are you?"

"I'm in the cottage."

"Stay where you are. I'll be there in five minutes."

Awash with relief, she whispered into the phone, "Just park out on the road so no one will hear you. I'll meet you out there."

"No! Stay in the cottage. I'll check the place out and come down to let you know what I find."

Irritation cracked in her mind like a whip, making her forget all about whispering and vulnerability. "I already checked the doors and windows. They're locked up tight. If someone's in there, they got in with a key."

"You what?" Outrage was evident in his voice. "Stay where you are, Gillian. I mean it!"

"Don't tell me what to do. Just get over here!" She was wet, cold, and miserable. Her toe was throbbing, and Seth was daring to give her orders. Not trusting herself to speak civilly, she slammed the receiver back into place on the wall. All she needed was for Seth to ride in on his white horse and save the day. Everybody's hero.

Hobbling as fast as possible through the darkened living

room, she worked her way to the door and rushed out into the rain once again. She had no clear plan, but there was no way she was going to sit around and wait for Seth to show up to rescue her.

Glancing over at Maude's house, she was relieved to see a light in the upstairs window. That meant the power in her own house would probably be restored, and Maude might actually be up. Now, she could risk getting the key back without causing the woman heart failure.

Changing course, she ran across the lawn and gingerly tiptoed across the gravel drive. Why hadn't she taken the time to put on some shoes? She rounded the corner to the front of Maude's house, and just as she climbed the stairs and prepared to knock, the door swung open.

Gillian screamed and jumped back from the door.

Maude stood in the doorway backlit by the inside lights, her features cast in shadow, looking more like an apparition than a flesh-and-blood woman in her flowing white robe. Her hair was wet and slicked back from her face, making her look harsh and angry, which she very probably was. "What are you doing out in the rain, girl? You'll catch your death."

At first, Gillian couldn't quite manage to get a sound out around her constricted vocal cords. Swallowing, she tried again. "I need the key to my shop, Mrs. Strickland."

"Whatever for? It must be past midnight, and there's a terrible storm out there," she said unnecessarily.

Soaked to the skin and shivering, Gillian gathered her patience. "I'm sorry to disturb you so late, but I think someone's inside the shop," she explained.

Mrs. Strickland was silent for a moment, then asked, "Why would someone be in the shop at this hour?"

Patience waning, Gillian resisted the urge to barge into Maude's house and get the key herself. "I don't know, but I'm going to find out. I need the key."

"Well, I don't know where I put it, and it's too late to

find it now. Come back in the morning." She stepped back and started to close the door, but Gillian caught it with a hand to prevent her from shutting it.

At Maude's angry glare, she snatched her hand back and tried to reason with her. "Mrs. Strickland, please. I need the key."

Maude shook her head. "I can't help you tonight. I told you I don't know where it is." With that, she slammed the door in Gillian's face.

Standing on the darkened porch with the door shut tightly against her, she couldn't remember a time when she felt more frustrated. She knew it was late and she'd probably frightened the woman by knocking on her door during a storm, but she couldn't believe how stubborn Maude had been. Suddenly Seth's version of his aunt became a lot more believable. Where was the sweet lady who'd spent the entire day helping her out without expecting anything in return?

Momentarily defeated, she sat down on the porch steps and did the only thing she could. She waited for Seth to arrive with his key.

Five minutes seemed like five hours, and she was in a foul mood by the time he arrived. When his truck finally pulled into the drive, lights off, Gillian was wet, cold, and more than ready to pick a fight.

"Where have you been?" she demanded, her voice hissing through bared teeth.

Ignoring her question, Seth grabbed her arm and gave her a little shake. "What are you doing out here? I told you to lock the doors and stay in the house."

Gillian snatched her arm from his grasp. "Don't you dare give me orders! I should have known you'd never change."

Seth growled in anger and took Gillian totally off guard as he grabbed her around the hips and hauled her over his shoulder. Before she could catch the breath that had been knocked out of her, he carried her halfway back to the cottage. Her struggles didn't hamper him in the least, and within moments she was unceremoniously dumped on her rump in a puddle on the rickety cottage steps.

Temper flaring, she reached out and grabbed Seth's shins as he turned and took his first step toward the shop. Like a giant oak, he fell face down into the muddy grass with a soft thud. Before he could recover, she was off like a shot across the lawn, casually waiting on the back steps when he finally caught up with her.

"Shhh!" she whispered, motioning to the door behind her. If he were going to kill her it would have to be later, after they checked things out.

Seth dug into his pocket and pulled out the key. Placing a finger to his lips, he motioned for Gillian to follow as he unlocked the kitchen door and stepped inside.

Quietly, they worked their way around the kitchen table to the hallway beyond, pausing to listen keenly before making their way to the living room at the front of the house. Gillian stood rooted to the spot as Seth wove his way through the china cabinets and highboys, listening for any sound that was out of place.

When Seth rejoined her, they did the same with the dining room and began the ascent up the stairs. Slowly, trying to avoid making the wood creak beneath their weight, they tiptoed to the top and stood silently listening. Hearing nothing unusual, they checked each of the four bedrooms, then went down into the dark and eerie basement. Finally, they went back up to the kitchen.

Seth flipped on the light switch, causing them both to squint in the sudden brightness. Recovering first, Gillian stepped over to the sink and dampened a paper towel to give to Seth.

"Wipe your face. You're a mess," she said, nervous laughter simmering just below the surface. The adrenaline rush had receded, leaving her standing on Jell-O legs.

He took the towel and wiped at the mud, but the towel

wasn't up to the task. Tossing it toward the trash can, he strode to the sink and washed up while Gillian stood watching. Turning toward her once more, he leaned back on the counter and raised a questioning brow.

Gillian felt the heat claim her face as she tried to gather her scattered wits. She couldn't have been mistaken about the light coming from within the house. And if there had been light from within, it had to have come from a flashlight or lantern, because the power had been out at the time.

"There was someone in here," she said, hating the shakiness she heard in her voice.

"There's no sign of forced entry," he reasoned.

"Someone was in here," she insisted.

"For what purpose?" he asked.

She threw her hands into the air and began to pace the length of the kitchen. "How should I know? It *is* an antique store, you know."

Seth howled at that. "Yeah, and everyone knows it's filled to the gills with garage-sale leftovers."

She bristled and stiffened her spine. "Well, we can expect that attitude out of everyone else because they haven't been in yet to see the transformation, but obviously you can't recognize valuable treasures when they're sitting directly beneath your nose." She walked over to the 1940s Sunbeam mixer sitting on the countertop. "Want to take a guess on it's worth?"

Seth shrugged. "Fifty bucks?"

"One-fifty."

She reached into the glass-front cabinet and took down a red tomato-footed teapot. "Another guess?"

"I'd pay to have it hauled off. That thing's ugly as sin."

"Royal Bayreuth. Three-fifty. If I had the sunflower milk pitcher, I could get twelve hundred."

Seth was incredulous. "Dollars? Twelve hundred dollars?"

She carefully placed both pieces back in the cabinet and

gently closed the door, then flashed him her best "I told you so" look. He certainly deserved it. While he'd been hammering away, replacing floorboards upstairs, hadn't he seen the transformation her shop had been undergoing? When she'd first come the place had been a mess, but she'd unearthed a wealth of lovely antiques. There was everything from Depression glass to silver and china, not to mention the beautiful pieces of oak, mahogany, maple, and cherry furniture that had been hiding beneath the clutter and dust. It hurt that he hadn't noticed.

"I'm going to go look again. Someone probably took off with the silver or something."

"It's late, Gillie." Seth stifled a yawn and reached for her as she passed, but she sidestepped him with determination.

Flipping on lights as she went, she stormed through every room looking for evidence of burglary, totally baffled when she found none. "I don't understand," she said wearily, sinking into one of the kitchen chairs. "I know I saw a flashlight beam in the upstairs window. I know someone was in here."

"Maybe it was the reflection of lightning in the distance," Seth offered.

Anger flared within her. Why would he doubt her? "I know what I saw."

Seth closed his eyes for a moment and ran his hand around the back of his neck. "Do you want to call Billy Watkins and have him look around?"

"No." She threw her hands up in frustration and dropped them limply to her sides. "There's nothing here for them to see, no proof that someone was here. They'll just think I frightened myself into believing I saw something."

Seth dropped his gaze and she knew that's what he thought. "Let me look around one more time before we call it a night," he offered, but she knew it was just to appease her.

Defeated for the moment, Gillian shook her head. "Don't

bother. No one's here now. Tomorrow morning's soon enough, I guess."

Seth cautiously approached and pulled her up into his arms for a hug. Unable to hold onto her anger, drained from the evening's events, Gillian settled against his chest, taking comfort in both the steady beat of his heart and his willingness to keep searching for clues even though he doubted what she'd seen.

After a few minutes, he hugged her tightly and dropped a kiss on her damp hair. "Come on, Sparky, let's get you home and into some clean, dry clothes."

She shoved against his chest halfheartedly, not really wanted to leave the warmth of his arms. "I hate that name, you know."

Seth tucked two fingers beneath her chin and tilted her face up to place a tender kiss on the little scar on her forehead. She shivered and felt her heart melt a bit more. "I know, but if anyone ever deserved it, it's you. You've got more spirit and fire in you than anyone I've ever known."

His eyes held hers captive for a heartbeat and her heart fluttered in her chest. She could lose herself in this man if she wasn't very careful. She could love him and let him take control of her life and lose all the backbone and self-reliance she'd worked so hard for all these years. As tempting as loving him was, she couldn't let that happen. He wasn't even staying around much longer anyway. If she knew what was good for her, she'd keep him at arm's length.

With willpower she didn't know she possessed, she pushed out of his arms and turned toward the window where she caught her reflection. "Ugh. You got me all muddy!"

Seth chuckled. "You got me muddy first. Now, let's go get you cleaned up and tucked into bed." Putting his arm around her shoulders, he steered her out the kitchen door and turned to lock it behind him.

Gillian shrugged off his arm. He sure wasn't making it easy to distance herself. "I can manage from here. You go on home."

"And leave you to get jumped when you go back to the cottage? Not a chance."

A shiver of apprehension raced up her spine. What if the intruder had entered her cottage while she was out searching for him? It couldn't hurt to have Seth check things out for her since he was here anyway. "Okay, have a look if it makes you feel better."

She didn't protest this time as he took her hand and walked her down. He had nice hands. Firm and warm. Safe. And she was cold from the rain, which had finally come to an end. The distant rumble of thunder and occasional drip of rain falling from the leaves were the only evidence of the recent storm.

Tentatively, he pushed open the cottage door and switched on the light, illuminating her living room where everything seemed to be in order. Then, he systematically searched the entire cottage with Gillian nearly plastered to his back, checking doors and windows, before declaring it safe and sound. Finally, they stood in the living room, both still muddy and damp, with nothing left to say.

"Well, I guess I'd better go change and get to bed. Thanks for coming out to help me."

He reached up and tucked a damp tendril of hair behind her ear. "You should dry your hair before you go back to bed. You don't want to get sick again."

She was perplexed. "I haven't been sick."

He frowned. "You were sick today, remember? You left early to lie down."

"Oh, that. I get migraines sometimes."

Seth looked concerned. "You do? Liz gets them. Sometimes it helps to have someone massage her temples and neck. Why don't you lie down on the couch and I'll see what I can do."

Gillian protested quickly, both intrigued and appalled by the idea of having his hands on her. "No, no! That's all right. I'm feeling much better now."

Seth persisted. "You're pale as a ghost, and you're looking strained around the eyes. Come over here and sit."

It was an order gently given, but an order nonetheless, and she was torn between obeying and defying him. Maude's talk about Seth taking charge of his family's lives had confused her, and she wasn't sure of his motives now. She only knew she didn't want to be vulnerable.

She was tired and confused, the remnants of her earlier headache still hovering in her head despite what she'd just told Seth. With the excitement of the past couple of hours thrown in, it was just too much to deal with right now. She snapped, "I don't need anything from you right now, okay? Just go home."

She watched his eyes as concern turned to hurt, but she wouldn't have yanked back the words if she could. She was becoming far too dependent on him and far too attracted. Attraction led to other things, like dating and kissing and . . . love. Flirting was one thing, falling in love quite another.

It was something she simply wasn't prepared to risk.

Her words were like a slap in the face. He'd only been offering to help, but she wasn't willing to accept it. Sure, she'd called him tonight, but she wouldn't have bothered if she hadn't needed the key. He'd never known a more stubborn, independent woman than this one. She wouldn't even allow herself a helping hand offered for no other reason than compassion. Bottom line was she might be attracted to him, but she didn't trust him, and without trust, where were they?

"Goodnight, Gillian. Get some sleep," he whispered, then walked out the door, shutting it firmly behind him.

Tires spit gravel as he wheeled the truck around in her

driveway and hit the highway toward home. He was angry with her, but even angrier with himself.

He'd built a wall around his heart and had guarded it well. Not once had he been in danger of falling in love. The last thing he needed was one more person depending on him. But when Gillian returned, she opened up a part of him he thought he'd closed away forever. A part that wanted to take a chance on happiness, try his hand at . . . what?

He didn't know what exactly. He only knew he wanted to trust her and to have her trust. He wanted to protect her and care for her.

So, maybe she was right to send him away, refuse his offer to help and comfort. They needed to put some distance between them before they did something stupid like fall in love. That could only be a mistake for them both.

Then, suddenly, there it was again . . . that restless feeling that slithered through his belly and made him count the days until freedom. He hadn't noticed it lately, but now he welcomed it and focused hard on his goal. He knew what he wanted and where he was going. Nothing was going to hold him back.

So then why, suddenly, did September loom a bit too close for comfort?

Chapter Ten

Aweek passed without a glimpse of Seth. Gillian knew he'd been working in the shop, most likely in the early morning or late evening hours. She'd seen a steady light burning in the upstairs windows several mornings as early as four o'clock and several nights as late as eleven. But as she looked around the room, the real evidence of his efforts was apparent in the beautiful details, such as the crown molding and chair rail he'd placed around the parlor and dining room ceiling and walls. The smell of fresh paint still lingered in the air but was dissipating daily with the help of the large fans Seth had left for her to use in the open windows. The place was more beautiful than she'd ever imagined it could be, largely due to Seth's thoughtfulness and skill at his craft. She couldn't have done it without him.

She missed him, but she'd made the decision to keep him at a distance, and she meant to stick to it. How easily she'd become accustomed to his presence in her life, how quickly she'd become attracted to him as much more than a friend.

She rearranged a cobalt blue vase of silk flowers on the beautifully crocheted scarf that graced the tiger oak parlor table and stepped back to assess the results. It was lovely, as were the rest of the pieces in the house, but it wasn't bringing her pleasure. Her heart was too heavy for that. She missed Seth.

With a sigh, she left the parlor, wandering aimlessly from room to room. For more than a month she'd worked nonstop to get the place up and running. Now, with opening day only a day away, she had nothing left to do but wait and worry.

Hoping some fresh air would help clear her mind, she poured some iced tea and went to rock on the front porch. The day was hot, but there was a slight breeze and it was comfortable in the shade.

Within moments, her peace was interrupted as Seth's pickup pulled into the drive. Before she could beat a hasty retreat, he was bounding up the porch steps like an eager puppy while she sat frozen as stiff as laundry left hanging on a January line.

"Hey, beautiful." He leaned down and planted a warm kiss on her forehead, which she felt all the way down to her toes. "What's new?"

Refusing to meet his eyes, she just shrugged. What did they really have to discuss anyway? She'd made her feelings perfectly clear the other night.

"What's wrong? Cat got your tongue?" He leaned down and kissed her cheeks, causing them to bloom.

She'd missed him so much during the past few days and now here he was acting as though nothing had happened, as if she hadn't pushed him away. And he'd put up crown molding for her. How had he known she'd love it?

"Iced tea?" she offered, weakening a bit. Keeping him away was just so hard. Maybe they'd get the friends thing right if they practiced a little more. If he could put it behind him, then she could too.

"Don't mind if I do." Encircling her wrist with his strong hand, he brought her glass closer and leaned in to take a sip. Then, using his other hand, he took the iced tea from her and laid her cool, wet hand against his warm cheek. "Friends?"

She pulled her hand away, holding it protectively in front of her, and nodded. "Friends." Then, because she needed a moment to think, she told him to sit while she went inside to pour him some tea.

Seth watched her go and wondered what had happened to his brain. If he had an ounce of common sense in his head, he'd tell her the job was done and he was here to collect his pay and nothing more. That's what he'd intended to do when he'd driven out here. If he had an ounce of backbone, he'd tell her to sell the shop now that it was fixed up and marketable and walk away before this town sucked her dry too. If he had a heart of steel, he'd tell her he didn't want her more than he wanted to take his next breath. Then, he'd walk away and never look back.

But he didn't have any of those things, it seemed, because instead, he followed her into the house.

Gillian entered the parlor just as he sat down on the settee. Her eyes were wary. "It's a nice day outside."

He chose to ignore her hint.

"I have something to say and it's private."

Wariness gave way to alarm. "Look, Seth, there's no reason to do that. I think we know where we stand here. You're leaving in a couple of months, so that's that."

He rose and took the iced tea from her hand, setting it on the nearest table, then took her hand and led her to the small couch. "Sit, Gillian."

She resisted. "Seth, I—"

"I came to get my pay and to bring these," he said, and pulled the treasure from his shirt pocket. He knew the instant she recognized what was in his hand, because her eyes went soft and she sank down onto the couch.

"My glasses," she cried. "Oh my gosh, Seth. You've had my glasses all these years?"

His only goal had been to make her understand he treasured their friendship, both past and present, and didn't want to do anything to hurt it. But when she looked at him that way with those gorgeous green eyes, he just couldn't help himself. He thought he'd die right on the spot if he didn't taste her lips right that minute and breathe in her delicate scent.

Throwing caution to the wind, he knelt before her and gently slipped his hands into her hair, bringing her close so they were eye to eye. "I need to kiss you," he said, and did just that.

Gillian's senses reeled. His kiss was as sweet as she'd dreamed it would be. She needed some distance and fast. With Seth so close, it was hard to regain her perspective. Just a short time ago, she'd had perfectly sound reasons for keeping their relationship on a platonic level, but at the moment, she couldn't recall a single one. "Seth, I . . ." she began, as she pulled slightly away, only to have Seth quiet her with a gentle hand over her mouth.

"Listen," he whispered.

Gillian silently shifted on the settee, angling her head. She didn't hear a thing but the steady pounding of her heart.

Suddenly, the jangling of her little brass bells had them both leaping to their feet, pretending they hadn't just shared a very enlightening kiss.

"I knocked," Maude said directly to Seth, then, with a pointed looked at Gillian, concluded disapprovingly, "but, I can see you were too busy to answer. I just came by to return your key."

"I would have liked to have gotten it back the other night when I needed it," Gillian replied.

Maude shrugged and let the key slip into Gillian's open

hand. "I'm finished with it now. Is there anything you need for your big day tomorrow? I'm on my way into town."

So this was the side of Aunt Maude that her nieces and nephews had warned her about. "Can't think of a thing."

Maude nodded, then shifted a gaze suddenly full of meaning to Seth. "I thought you were through here."

Seth ran a hand through his hair and sighed. "Just tying up some loose ends, Aunt Maude."

Maude pursed her lips, considering. "Looks to me like you're stirring them up. Are you sure you know what you're doing?"

There was a moment's silence before Seth replied, a pause during which Gillian waited with bated breath. Then he shook his head and reached for Gillian, pulling her into a gentle embrace. "I have no earthly idea."

Gillian remembered his tender kiss, and with a delicious little shiver realized she felt the same way. She had no idea what she was doing, but whatever it was it felt wonderful.

Maude's silence said more than any words she could have uttered and she punctuated it with the slam of the door behind her.

"You gave her a key?" Seth hugged Gillian closer, then held her slightly away.

"It was only supposed to be for one night."

"Which night?"

"That night."

He groaned. "You don't think . . ." His words trailed off, but he didn't have to finish for Gillian to understand where he was headed.

"No!" she exclaimed, "No. Maude wouldn't have . . . well, she couldn't have . . . surely you don't think . . ."

Seth shrugged. "I'm not sure what to think, but I told you she was up to something. Just keep an eye on her, okay, and call me if you need me again."

"I will," she promised, wondering just what Maude was capable of.

He pulled away and went back to sit down on the settee, patting the spot next to him in an invitation for Gillian to join him there. When she complied, he took her hand and gave it a squeeze. "There's a lot you don't know about my family, Gillian, and it's a bit overwhelming, especially for someone who comes from a small family, to take in. I promise to tell you all about it, but first we need to talk about more important things."

She squeezed her eyes shut and shook her head, wishing the earth would simply open up and swallow her whole. It was one thing to acknowledge her feelings to herself, another thing entirely to say them aloud to Seth.

He kissed her cheek and cupped her chin, bringing her face up to his. "Too late to hide now, kid. We've gotta get it out in the open." He ran a hand through her hair and cupped the back of her head, then rested his forehead upon hers. "I don't want to hurt you. That's why I walked away last time, but I can't stay away." He cupped her face and looked directly into her eyes, the sincerity of his words evident in his gaze.

She was touched by the truth of his words. He wasn't professing undying love. He wasn't saying he'd stay or that he'd love her forever. Instead, he was being completely honest with her, and she could do nothing but offer the same in return. "That's exactly how I feel."

He kissed her tenderly, deeply, then sighed. "So what do we do about it?"

Tears stung her eyes and she blinked, letting them fall and land where they would. What she wanted to do and what she should do were definitely two different things.

"There's not much we can do about it, is there? I think we should just be what we always were. Very, very good friends."

His hand fell from her face, leaving the ghost of his touch behind. He rose from the settee and extended a hand to her. "Then that's what we'll do. Let's go get something to eat, friend."

Gillian forced a smile around the tears in her heart and took his hand. She'd offered friendship, and she planned to make good on it, but as she settled into his pickup a few moments later and watched as he walked around to the driver's side, she wondered if they'd ever be able to pull it off.

Twenty minutes later, they were sitting at a window table at the diner, glancing over the menus Suzie had set out for them. She'd guided them to a booth near the back that afforded them some privacy, though the place was unusually quiet, even for late afternoon. They placed their orders, and within a few minutes, Seth was sinking his teeth into a gigantic, juicy hamburger brimming with ketchup and Gillian was picking through a huge platter of Southern fried chicken salad.

Gillian was the first to break the silence. "Heather and Kaylee are coming to my opening tomorrow. They're beautiful girls."

"Like their sister. Patty told me your visit went well."

Gillian displayed mock outrage. "Talking about me again? Does your meddling know no bounds?"

Seth cocked his head, as though considering, then explained, "I come by it honestly. On my mother's side of the family it's as natural as eating and breathing."

Gillian grinned slyly. "So you admit you meddle."

He shrugged. "Yeah. When you've got a family like mine, you either do it or have it done to you. Besides, with Lizzie and Jackson running around aimlessly all the time, someone's got to lay down the law and offer some guidance. It pays to know what's going on so I can head off trouble."

"From Liz and Jackson?" At his nod, she asked, "Isn't that their parents' problem?"

"Their mom passed away years ago after a long, rough battle with cancer. My mom sort of took them under her wing, but then she passed away." The pain of the loss was evident in Seth's face.

"I'm so sorry," Gillian said softly, feeling inadequate at comforting him.

"That's just the way it is. Anyway, my cousins aren't the only ones worth watching. Maude's always causing mischief as well."

"I'm beginning to believe that," she said, thinking of how Maude had refused to return her key that stormy night. Maybe she should have the locks changed.

"I'm sorry about the way she barged in today."

Gillian considered that for a moment. "Don't be. It was for the best." What would have happened if she hadn't?

Seth seemed to mull that over. "Not from where I'm sitting."

She pushed her salad away and ignored his comment. "Tell me more."

"Maude seems to want to make the rest of us as unhappy as she's always been. I'm an easy mark since I'm *in charge.* Everything that goes wrong is automatically my fault in Aunt Maude's eyes."

Gillian laughed at the absurdity of that, a little jealous that she didn't have family with which to have little squabbles, then smiled when she remembered Heather and Kaylee. Maybe they'd have squabbles some day too. "Does she also blame you for the rain and snow?"

"She would if she could, I imagine. She's been a bitter woman all my life. I don't think she knows what happiness is." Seth wiped his hands, then reached into his pocket and pulled out some bills which he threw on the table. "Come on, Sparky, let's roll."

"And what do you know about happiness? You've spent the better part of the last eight years bellyaching about how miserable you are around here." Suzie's comment caught them both off guard, and Gillian cast a quick glance at Seth, wondering what his reaction would be. "He's been quite the gentleman since you arrived, Gillian, but he's usually as surly as a hungry bear."

Gillian laughed as Suzie cleared the dishes from the table, then wiped it clean, sending most of the crumbs flying onto Seth's lap.

"Hey, Suz! What's that for?" Seth stood and brushed the crumbs from his lap, then gave Suzie's arm a playful flick of his finger.

"That's for airing family laundry in public. I could hear you all the way over at the counter. Makes me wonder what you say about me behind my back."

Gillian watched with amusement as Seth turned on his charm. "Now, Suzie, you know I love you. You're my favorite cousin, remember? Besides, your daddy would have my backside in a sling if he thought I was spreading rumors about this year's Macon County Ruby Queen." He grabbed her hand and brought it to his lips, but she snatched it back before he could land a kiss.

"That's right, cousin, and don't you forget it. Now, where's Jackson been keeping himself? He hasn't been in since y'all were here for lunch."

Seth shrugged. "I dunno. I haven't seen him all week. Maybe he and Elizabeth finally did each other in and no one's found their bodies yet."

Gillian laughed, but Suzie socked Seth in the shoulder, sending him reeling a couple of steps backwards. "That's not funny, Seth. I won't have you talking badly about them anymore in this diner. They're good people and they're family, so just stop washing your dirty laundry in public and show them the respect they're due, do you hear?" Then she flung her wet rag at him and ran into the kitchen, the double doors swinging madly behind her.

Biting her lip to keep the laughter from spilling forth, Gillian watched Seth struggle to understand his cousin's outburst. Finally, when she couldn't stand it another moment and it was apparent he just didn't get it, she said, "I think maybe Suzie has feelings for Jackson."

Seth started to deny it, she could tell, but then thought better of it. "Suzie and Jackson?"

Gillian nodded.

"My Suzie?"

She nodded again.

"My Jackson?"

Once again, she gave a slow nod. It was fascinating the way life could dance around a man without him being aware.

Seth looked at the now-still kitchen doors, then back at Gillian. "Do you think?"

She grinned and simply arched a brow. It was a woman thing, she supposed. "I told you so before. Don't worry yourself over it, Seth. It'll all work out the way it's supposed to, and you really don't have to get involved if you don't want to. They're grownups and they can take care of themselves."

He grunted. "If you say so, but . . ."

"They'll be fine," she assured him.

Seth followed as she led the way out the door and into the hot July sunshine. "What time is your opening tomorrow?"

"Ten o'clock." She sighed, feeling the butterflies fluttering about in her stomach. "But what if no one comes?"

"They'll come," he assured her. "If for no other reason than to see what you've done with the place, and, of course, for free food."

Gillian smiled at that. "I suppose that's true. I hope I have enough for everyone."

Seth laughed. "First you're worried they won't come, and then you're worried you won't be able to feed them all. They'll start with hot dogs at the hardware store, pizza at the drugstore, soft drinks and doughnuts at the Piggly

Wiggly, chocolate cake at the furniture store, candy at the craft store. They'll be ripe for cookies and tea by the time they get to you." In an agile move, he opened the truck door for her and, at the same time, placed his arm around her shoulders and pulled her close, then playfully nipped at her ear.

If he was trying to distract her, it was certainly working. Goosebumps shivered up and down her arms as she half-heartedly tried to pull away. "Stop it, Seth," she protested weakly, tingling from his touch. "That's a bit friendlier than I had in mind."

With a final little nip on her neck, he agreed. "Yeah, I know. Just friends."

Chapter Eleven

What a day, Seth thought, as he headed back toward the hardware store a little later. It must have been a dream. A week ago, he'd been trying to avoid her, put her from his mind, and now she was all he could think about. A week ago, he'd been confused.

He wasn't confused now. He knew exactly how he felt about her. He just didn't know what he was supposed to do about it. For now, he enjoyed her company and that would have to do. What was there to know, other than that?

It was a very optimistic man who entered Valley Hardware, and Elizabeth was the first to notice the change.

"You must have had a good time last night, Seth," she commented. "I haven't seen that look on your face since you took both the Thompson twins to Octoberfest two years ago."

"I only had a date with one of them. The other one tagged along when her date stood her up, and you know it," he replied dryly.

"Yeah, but they both got married by spring, so both of them counted," she reasoned.

He hated being reminded of his old reputation. He hadn't dated anyone in over a year, but the talk just didn't die down. "Liz, I'd appreciate it if you'd keep that sort of information to yourself from now on. No need to go spreading rumors based on half-truths."

"Then tell me the whole truth," she demanded softly, a commanding look in her eyes. "Tell me you're not involved with Gillian."

Seth felt a moment's discomfort at the reminder of his reputation. What he felt for Gillian was more than he'd felt for anyone else, and he didn't want her compared with the women of his past. "You worried about her?"

Elizabeth pursed her lips and studied her shoes for a few seconds before lifting her eyes to his. "Yes, I guess I am. I wouldn't want to see her get hurt with her just getting settled in and all. The other women you've known went into the relationships with their eyes open." She shrugged delicately. "Gillian could get blindsided."

Guilt, swift as a hunter's arrow, pierced his heart, and he lashed out before he could stop himself. "You better watch out there, Lizzie. If you're not careful, someone might think you care."

Seth unlocked the safe and took out the moneybags for the cash registers. He placed them on the desk and checked the contents of each. They had plenty of cash on hand for their day, which was good since the banks were closed for the holiday.

Now, he really wanted Elizabeth to back off so he could leave the office and get on with his day, but when he tried to leave, she stood in his way. "Move, Mary Elizabeth!"

She couldn't have looked more stunned. "Mary Elizabeth? You haven't called me that since I was sixteen and you caught me smoking in the dugout at Bradley field. Hit a nerve, did I?"

"I'm through playing games with you. I've got to get to work so I can get on over to Gillian's grand opening. I told her I'd be there before noon."

Elizabeth dug her purse out of the desk drawer and rummaged through it for a moment, then produced a crumpled piece of paper. "Why don't you leave Gillian alone, Seth. Let some nice local fellow court her and marry her once she's had a chance to get settled in. I've got a girlfriend who's dying to go out with you." She handed the paper to Seth. "Here's her number. Think about it."

Seth ripped the paper in half and tossed it in the nearby trash can. He knew the rumors that circulated about him. The love 'em and leave 'em bachelor. It had never bothered him until now. Until Gillian. Would people see her as just another one of his conquests?

Then, another thought occurred to him. A thought he liked even less. When he was gone, would she marry the first man who came along behind him? He frowned at the thought. Gillian in another man's arms was not something he wanted to envision. In fact, if he didn't know better, he'd think he was jealous.

Jealous? That was ridiculous. He wasn't jealous. He just didn't like to think of her being with someone else while they were involved. Not that they were exactly involved in anything except friendship. He mulled that over for a moment, and then, satisfied that he had a handle on it, made a decision. He'd make sure she knew their friendship was exclusive for as long as it lasted, and he didn't care what she did after that.

"Seth?" Elizabeth interrupted his turbulent thoughts. "Where have you been? Did you hear a word I said?"

Honesty was the best policy, he decided. "Not a word, brat."

"You've got a look about you that's totally different from any I've ever seen, and that worries me, Seth. I just don't want to see either one of you get hurt when you leave."

"You don't have to worry about her hurting me, Lizzie. I'm a big boy. I know how to take care of myself. If anything, Gillian's the one who stands to be hurt, but I'm going to try my hardest to avoid that."

"You know what they say. When you play with fire, you're bound to get burned." She stepped around him and left the office, shutting the door softly behind her.

Her parting words had had an ominous ring to them that dampened his spirit. With a dismissive grunt, he gathered up the moneybags and left the office to prepare for the day.

He certainly didn't want to waste a moment worrying about Elizabeth's warning. There was no way he was going to get burned . . . was there?

Opening day was a huge success already, and it wasn't yet noon. When Gillian had gone up to the shop to prepare for the day, there'd been customers sitting in the rocking chairs on her porch waiting for her. She'd quickly opened her office and booted up her computer, which would keep track of sales, then unlocked the cash box, just in case she actually *made* a sale. Then, she'd turned on the CD player so that the tinkling sounds of a piano softly floated throughout the house. Finally, she'd unlocked the front door and greeted her customers, who'd turned out to be friends of Katie's mom. Remembering the cookies and tea, she'd run back to the kitchen to get them, and put some coffee on to brew as well.

That had been at nine o'clock. It was now almost eleven-thirty, and she'd barely had time to think of anything other than being a hostess since she'd opened the front doors. Her worries that no one would show proved to be unfounded, as did her worries that people would only come for the food. There were still cookies on the platters, though she'd had to refill the tea twice and brew another pot of coffee, but her customers were definitely more interested in her merchandise than in the food.

So far, she'd sold several pieces of depression glass and a forty-five-piece place setting of Desert Rose china that she hadn't been sure would ever sell in the first place. Her furniture was being "oohed" and "aahed" over, and she felt pride in the job she'd done on it. She'd worked hard and fast refinishing a few pieces while Seth and his buddies fixed up the place for the opening. Seth had been helpful moving the pieces down to her basement, then back up again when they were finished. She'd never have been able to pull this off without his help.

"This dresser's mine, you know. I've been looking all over for it."

Maude Strickland jolted Gillian out of her reflections and she looked at the piece in question. It was one of the pieces she'd recently refinished down in the basement. In fact, it was the one the letter had fallen out of. Now *that* was interesting. "It was down in the basement, so I refinished it. It's a beautiful piece. How did it come to be in Mr. Keeney's possession?"

"Seth sold it to him, the nitwit. He cleaned out the barn for me and sold all of the old junk to Edward. I could have wrung his neck that day."

Gillian felt terrible. Why would Seth have sold the piece without asking Maude's permission first? "Did you receive a fair price for it, Mrs. Strickland?"

"Fair enough, but I didn't want the money. I told Edward I'd return the money, but he wouldn't hear of it." She eyed Gillian with derision. "Then you came."

The piece was in solid shape now that Gillian had taken it apart piece by piece and restored it to its natural beauty. She could make several hundred dollars on it, which would get her on her way toward purchasing an air conditioner for the shop, but the look of longing on Maude's face was too much to bear. "I'll sell it back to you at the price you paid, if you'd like."

Maude sniffed. "That's a fine offer, but I don't need it anymore."

Gillian smiled. "If it was sold without your knowledge,

then you should have it back—at no cost. Consider it payment for all the work you did for me."

Maude's eyes took on a faraway look as she ran her hand
over the smooth oak surface. A frown marred her features.
"This was the dresser I took with me when I moved to
Atlanta. Mother and Daddy weren't pleased that I wanted
to attend college there. They wanted me to stay put and
marry my high school sweetheart, but I had dreams. Big
dreams. I was going to leave this tired little town behind
and never come back." Her eyes met Gillian's and she suddenly looked ten years older than she had just a moment
before. "It was the biggest mistake I ever made."

Gillian searched Maude's faded eyes and saw pain in
their depths. It touched a chord within her, and for a moment, she knew Maude's pain. It was the pain of lost love,
of failure. It was the pain of years that had slipped through
open fingers like so much sand. As clear as a teardrop, she
knew that Maude had written the lost letter.

Gillian looked around the crowded shop and knew she
couldn't retrieve it now, but she wanted to return the letter
to Maude as soon as possible. "Aunt Maude, I have something special to give you later. Will you be home this afternoon after closing? I'd like to drop by for just a minute
before we leave for the carnival."

Maude nodded. "Until six. That's when Katie is picking
me up."

Gillian smiled tenderly and impulsively hugged the startled older woman. "I'll be there," she promised, then pulled
a sold tag out of the top drawer and attached it to the
drawer pull. "And I'll have Seth deliver this to you."

The morning swept away, and Gillian stayed busy ring-
ing up sales and meeting new people. No one was in a
huge hurry, with it being a holiday, and so she found people
making themselves comfortable on her porch, sipping tea
and eating cookies. Everyone was friendly, and some made

a point of telling her that they remembered her and her family, though only a few were familiar to Gillian.

When Patricia, Heather, and Kaylee came to wish her well, she thought she'd burst with pure happiness. How amazing that two girls she'd never even heard of could take a place of such importance in her heart and life. With pride, she gave them a tour of the shop, refusing to take their money when they found trinkets they wanted to buy. Heather fell in love with a lovely cameo brooch, and Kaylee unearthed a rusty, broken croquet set, proving that one man's trash truly was another man's, or girl's, treasure. Gillian tried to get Patricia to take a brooch to match Heather's, but she seemed uncomfortable with the idea and Gillian didn't want to push her. Maybe she'd wrap it up and give it to her for Christmas. And that thought brought another smile to her lips. She'd be sharing Christmas with family.

By two, she found the shop devoid of customers and her stomach devoid of food. Luckily, Seth chose that moment to arrive, and better yet, he had food in hand. With a flourish, he presented first the bag of burgers, then a dainty bouquet of black-eyed Susans—complete with dirty roots— he'd purloined from somewhere, most likely Maude's garden.

The sight of him sent a thrill straight to her toes. She wasn't even miffed that he was late. "It was wonderful," she declared, anxious to share the news about her morning as they spread their lunch out on the kitchen table.

"I agree," he said. "I can't wait to do it again."

Confused, Gillian asked, "What?"

"Kissing you," he replied with wide-eyed innocence. "What are *you* talking about?"

She could feel the blush steal across her cheeks. "I was talking about my grand opening, and you know it."

He winked. "I know. I just wanted to get a rise out of you," he teased. "Tell me about your day."

How wonderful to have somebody who cared. Years had gone by since anyone cared what she did unless it brought more money to the business. When money was involved, her mother cared. Thoroughly enjoying the moment, she told him every little detail she could remember, every little snippet of conversation she could recall. And he listened, without interrupting her once. Finally, she came back down from her high, flustered to find she'd been rambling on for over twenty minutes, but thrilled to see she still held his attention.

"You're a good listener," she said, somewhat surprised, trying to ignore the fluttering of her heart.

"You're an expressive storyteller," he replied. "I've always loved to listen to your stories and watch your face light up when you tell them."

The flutters turned to full-blown flapping as her heart took flight. "It's your turn," she said.

"I don't know any stories."

"Tell me about your day," she insisted.

"There's not much to tell." Wiping his mouth with a napkin, he stood and cleared the remains of their lunch off the table.

"Something must have happened at your store, Seth," she said. "You're later than you thought you'd be."

His expression closed just as tightly as a door shutting between them. "It was a busy day for us too. I told you I'd get here as soon as I could."

Gillian wasn't sure what had just happened. She hadn't been complaining about his time of arrival. She had just wanted to hear about his day and be as good a listener for him as he'd been for her. And she told him as much.

His eyes warmed again, and he pulled her into his arms for a kiss. It was a friendly kiss, rather than a passionate one, but no less potent than his other kiss had been. What would it be like to wake up to kisses this sweet every morning or to claim a quick one when he came home at the end of the day?

We're just friends, we're just friends, she repeated to herself, trying desperately to believe it was true, knowing it was a bald-faced lie.

"I'd better get back to the store before Jackson misses me. I told him I was going out for lunch, but I didn't tell him I was going this far out. He's probably ready to kill me long about now," he said as he released her and set her back on her feet. "You going to be ready to go to the carnival by five?"

"Most likely," she replied. "I don't think I'll get much late-afternoon business since folks will probably be getting ready to go to the carnival themselves."

"Especially since the cookies are long gone," Seth teased. Then, grasping her hand, he pulled her after him. "Come on, woman, walk me to the door."

"I'm giving Maude her dresser back this afternoon. Do you think you could take it over in your truck when you come to get me?"

He shook his head. "She gave me permission to sell the Keeneys that dresser, you know. Then she turned around and gave me grief for doing it. He paid her a pretty penny for it too." He tucked his hands in his jeans' pockets and looked over toward Maude's house. "I think she's insane."

"Not insane, Seth. In love."

His expression was enough to make Gillian chuck him gently on the shoulder. "Knock it off, Seth. She's entitled to her feelings, whatever they may be. Now, will you move the dresser today or do I have to hire Katie's sons to come and move it for me?"

Seth looked pained. "Heaven forbid. You put too much work into it to let those misfits touch it. I'll do it."

A quick kiss on the cheek was his reward. "Good. Now go on before Jackson sends out the posse to find you."

"Wear something pretty," he said, then was off the porch and in his truck backing from her drive before she could think of a suitable reply. Her heart was flopping around like a fish out of water. She wasn't sure what to expect from their friendship over the next few weeks, but the night ahead sure held a lot of promise.

Chapter Twelve

Afew hours later, Seth's whistle was as slow and appreciative as his gaze as it swept over Gillian from head to toe. Her auburn curls hung loose and wild about her nearly bare shoulders, tempting him to run his fingers through them to see if they were as soft as they looked. Her dress was frilly and flirty, just as he'd thought it might be. He felt a tug of possessiveness in a corner of his heart, but put it down to the fact that she was breathtakingly beautiful and all his—for the time being.

Gillian reached up and kissed him chastely on the cheek. "Thank you for the compliment."

He took the key from her and locked the cottage door, then took her hand in his and escorted her to his truck. As he opened the door for her, he placed his hand on her arm when she would have climbed inside. "You kept your promise."

"What promise?"

Seth gave in to temptation and ran his fingers down her hair. "You look very pretty."

Gillian shrugged delicately. "It's the least I could do. You're on time. Now let's get Maude's dresser delivered."

He'd remembered, but had hoped she'd forget. He didn't

want Maude to dampen the evening. "She told me to sell everything in the barn. I think you should have charged her for it."

"I tried, but she wouldn't buy it back, so I'm giving it to her."

He was totally perplexed. "Now what kind of logic is that?"

"So I'm a romantic," she said. "The dresser holds more meaning for her than you realize."

"Women," he said with a sigh, but he did as he was told and hauled the dresser out to his truck and over to Maude's house.

Maude was about as gracious receiving the dresser as a tax evader receiving an audit, but when Gillian pulled an old, folded envelope out of her purse and handed it to Maude, the older woman's eyes misted up and she hugged Gillian tightly. "Thank you," she cried, tears running unchecked down her cheeks.

Seth was amazed and terribly uncomfortable. In his twenty-eight years he'd never seen his aunt shed a tear. Helplessly, he stood to the side, then when it showed no sign of letting up, he retreated to the safety of the truck cab. "Women," he said, then sighed, totally baffled by the entire gender.

A few minutes later Gillian opened the cab door and climbed in with misty eyes and a mysterious smile.

Seth didn't even bother to ask as he pulled out onto the highway. There were some things men just weren't meant to understand. This was obviously one of them.

After a few minutes of riding in silence, he reached across the back of the seat to toy with Gillian's curls. He couldn't seem to get enough of their fiery softness. In a way, they represented Gillian herself: fiery temper, soft heart. It was a heart he'd seen her use to turn Maude around back there. He found himself reluctant to hurt that heart, lest he feel the heat of her temper.

"What's got you so quiet?" she asked.

"You," he replied honestly. "You take my breath away."

Gillian reached up and captured his hand, lacing her fingers with his, then brought it down to rest in her lap. "The feeling's mutual. Now, tell me what to expect tonight."

Something that had been nagging at him suddenly surged to the forefront. "Gillie, there's something I should tell you . . ."

She squeezed his hand. "That sounds ominous."

He chuckled uneasily, wondering how in the world to prepare Gillian for what could very possibly lie ahead, and pulled his hand away. "I guess I meant for it to."

"Just tell me," she urged, and he could feel her eyes on him. He felt like a dog.

"I've dated a lot of the local girls," he snapped, wondering when he'd become so defensive about it.

Gillian was silent for a full ten seconds, then burst out with a fit of laughter, punctuated by occasional unladylike snorts he'd once thought were adorable but now found extremely irritating. It took a few moments for her to gather herself sufficiently to speak. "And your point is?"

Whatever he'd expected her to say, it hadn't been that. "So you might hear things."

"Wonderful! What kind of things?" Her laughter said she was thoroughly enjoying herself.

"Nothing. Forget I said anything."

Gillian looked instantly remorseful. "You're sweet to worry about me, but I can hold my own against your old flames."

He was silent for a moment, then said sheepishly, "It sounds pretty juvenile, doesn't it?"

"Do they do fight over you on a regular basis?" she said teasingly.

Seth had the grace to flush. He'd come off as an egotistical jerk. "Yeah, at least once a week. We're here."

He turned the truck into the fairground entrance, found

a spot to park, and killed the engine. Before she could un-buckle and open her door, he cupped the back of her neck and pulled her over for a kiss. Then, when she made no move to do so herself, he unbuckled her seatbelt for her, walked around to open her door, and pulled her into his arms for another.

A sigh full of satisfaction escaped her as she muttered, "Yeah, I'll just bet they do fight over you. But they don't have to worry about me, Seth. We're just friends, remember?"

Seth threw his head back and laughed as he escorted her toward the ticket booth. *Just friends in big trouble,* he thought, but he wisely kept his opinion to himself.

Gillian was dazzled. The carnival was everything she'd imagined a carnival would be. Loud and noisy, it came complete with a double Ferris wheel, Tilt-a-whirl, Scrambler, Zipper, and fun house. But it was the game booths where Seth won her the stuffed teddy bear and necklace with two gold-filled charms that said "forever friends" that charmed her, and the elephant ears and cotton candy, which she shared with Seth, that tempted her.

As though he knew this was her first time at an old-fashioned carnival, he held her hand to hold her back, to make her savor each experience, when she would have rushed ahead from one thing to the next.

"Slow down, sweetheart, slow down," he cautioned. "There's no need to rush. We have all night."

Giddy with excitement and too much sugar, Gillian hugged him close with abandon and his arms encircled her, holding her tight. When they slowly pulled apart, Gillian felt like the world had turned upside down. Only Seth was in perfect focus. As long as she lived, she didn't think she'd ever forget this night and this moment.

He wrapped his arms around her again and held her close, his chin resting on her head. "Don't think, Gillian.

Just enjoy what life's offering right now at this moment. Tomorrow will take care of itself."

Would it? She wondered.

"Gillian! Seth!" They pulled apart and turned to find Heather working her way toward them through the crowd. "Have you seen Kaylee?" she asked when she drew near. "She was supposed to wait for me by the Tilt-a-Whirl but she wasn't there when I got off."

Gillian put a comforting arm around her sister. "How long has it been since you've seen her?"

Heather shrugged. "Maybe ten minutes. I don't know."

"Where's your mom?" Seth asked calmly, meeting Gillian's eyes over the girl's head and silently reminding her to stay calm for Heather's sake.

"Mom's working the cake booth for the church right now. Kaylee and I were supposed to stick together until she'd finished at nine. I wanted to ride some rides, but Kaylee felt sick to her stomach. She was supposed to wait for me."

Gillian took a deep breath to clear her mind. "So she's not riding rides or eating junk food. That leaves livestock and games."

"Games," Heather and Seth said in unison.

"She wanted to win a stuffed animal like you've got there," Heather said, pointing to the bear tucked beneath Gillian's arm, "but Mom told her not to waste her money. Those games are rigged."

That's exactly what Gillian had told Seth as he forked over the money to knock the bowling pins over with a little ball, but he'd won and she'd had to eat her words. They'd gone down exceptionally well with a candied apple. "Let's head that way and see if she's there. If not, we'll need to go find your mom."

Together they walked the length of the midway to the other end where the games were set up. Seth scanned one side and Gillian the other, keeping Heather safely tucked between them. The last thing they needed was to lose her too.

"There she is!" Heather cried, and they all turned to watch as Kaylee struggled to lift a sledgehammer over her shoulder, then let it plop harmlessly to a platform that was supposed to send a metal ball hurtling toward a bell attached to the top. The ball didn't move more than an inch.

"One more swing," the carnie called, "but you have to put some muscle into it."

Kaylee wore a look of sheer determination as she lifted the hammer over her head and tried again. The ball went no higher than it had the first time. Determination gave way to disappointment as the carnie took the hammer from her hands.

"Next!" he called, and handed the hammer to the next person in line.

Gillian walked over to her little sister and was about to put her arm around her when another girl gave Kaylee a little shove on the arm. "Your turn's over, loser. Move out of the way so my dad can win me something."

Quickly, Gillian slid her arm around Kaylee, but it was to restrain, not comfort. "Hold on, Kaylee. She's not worth it," Gillian whispered in her ear just as the bell clanged, announcing that the other girl's father had, indeed, won her a prize. When the girl stuck her tongue out at Kaylee, Gillian held on tight and Seth stepped up just in time.

"Which animal do you want, Kaylee?" he asked, as he fished a bill out of his wallet. "I can hit it once for a small one, twice for a medium one, or three times for a big one." He winked at her. "Your wish is my command."

Kaylee beamed and, with a glance at the brat and her head held high, placed all of her confidence in Seth. "A big one."

He grinned. "A big one it is."

Gillian held her breath and prayed he'd be successful, since the bratty girl was rooted to the spot, watching their every move. Seth picked up the hammer, lifted it high above his head, and let it fall. BAM, ring! BAM, ring! BAM, ring! Cheers went up throughout the crowd as the carnie hauled down a huge stuffed gorilla and handed it to Kaylee.

"Thanks, Seth," Kaylee cried, hugging her prize in a death grip.

"My pleasure, sweetheart," he said, draping an arm around her shoulders. "What else would you like for me to win for you tonight? Take your pick."

Kaylee pointed toward the bowling-pin booth where Seth had won Gillian's little bear, and they headed off in that direction with Heather on their trail. Gillian looked back at the bratty girl and her father and was pleased to see her pouting as her father shook his head "no." Obviously, her little stuffed dog wasn't as pleasing to her as it had been a few short minutes ago.

Gillian grinned and made a tally mark in the air. "Strike up one for the underdog," she said to no one in particular, then hurried along to catch up with the others, her heart swelling with pride, admiration, and—heaven help her— love for Seth.

After three more game booths both Kaylee and Heather had their arms full of stuffed animals and it was time to return them to their mother.

"Thanks again, Seth," Kaylee said, adoration shining in her eyes. "That was fun!"

Seth ruffled her hair, then Heather's. "It sure was, but I don't know what you two are gonna do with all those animals. Open a zoo?"

Patty, who'd just finished her shift at the bake sale booth, jangled her car keys. "They're going in the trunk right now, but I can guarantee they'll have a place of honor on their beds tonight." She gave Seth a quick hug and patted him on the back. "Thanks for taking care of them tonight. I know you had other things you'd have liked to do."

"They're wonderful girls, just like their mother." He put an arm around Patty, then one around Gillian. "And their sister."

"You're a charmer, Seth, but I don't have time for your sweet talk. It's almost time for the fireworks."

He glanced at his watch, then grabbed Gillian's hand. "We've got to get to the ferris wheel."

"But what about the fireworks?" she asked, as he pulled her along behind her.

Twenty minutes later, with the twinkling lights of the midway below them and the burst of brilliant fireworks above, Gillian had her answer. They had the best seats in the house.

Seth put his arm around her and pulled her close as the wind whipped around them with each turn of the wheel. Never in her life had she felt so alive, so carefree, so happy. Seth's words rang ominously in her mind. *Tomorrow will take care of itself.* She found herself wishing it could be tonight forever, but all too soon the show and the ride were over, and they were delivered back down to earth.

Gillian was fairly shimmering with excitement and struggled to find just the right words to express her happiness. "Seth, that was beautiful." It wasn't what she wanted to say, exactly, but it would have to do for now.

Seth cupped her face in his hands and looked deeply into her eyes. "You're beautiful," he whispered, as his mouth claimed hers in a tender kiss. "Let's go home."

Chapter Thirteen

Mr. Delaney's rooster crowed in the new day a wee bit sooner than Seth would have liked. A good two hours sooner. It was only six o'clock and he didn't have to be in to the hardware store until eight. Now that he was awake though, he figured he might as well go ahead and get up. If he went back to sleep, he'd just have more torturous dreams about Gillian.

Her face, alive with excitement, flashed into his mind and his heart constricted. She was so full of life and love. He'd had a difficult time dropping her off at her cottage and leaving her last night.

He quickly threw on his clothes and tucked his feet into his work boots, then headed into town to have breakfast at the diner. He needed a diversion fast because he was seriously considering taking his chances and driving out to her place to roust her out of bed.

As his truck neared her drive he slowed, wondering if he had the willpower to head on past, but in the end, he floored the gas pedal and peeled off, leaving telltale marks behind him. Seth was many things, but above all, he was honest with himself. And quite honestly, he knew he was in trouble. Big trouble.

* * *

139

The hardware store's glass doors swung open, drawing Seth's attention away from the catalog he was leafing through at the front register. The sight of Patty and the girls coming through the doors was as welcome as a breath of fresh air. He needed something to get his mind off one particular redhead. Hammers and nails just weren't doing the job.

"We weren't sure you'd be here so early. Thought you might have chosen to sleep in after last night," Patty said, leaning against the counter, looking prettier and younger than she had in years. The girls looked happier too, and he had to wonder if it was Gillian who'd brought some sunshine back into their lives.

"Someone had to come in and run the store. You know Elizabeth won't show her face today and Jackson's only good for stocking shelves." He shrugged helplessly and put on a "poor me" expression that earned him the girls' laughter.

"Well, the girls wanted to thank you again for winning all those stuffed animals last night and to issue an invitation. We were just going to leave it here for you, but since you're here, Kaylee can give it to you herself. It's really from her."

Kaylee produced a quarter-folded piece of blue construction paper. On the front it read: "Annual Camp Girls' Father-Daughter Dance," and on the inside it gave the date, place, and time. Seth wasn't sure what to say.

Patty must have sensed his hesitation. "You don't have to make a decision now. The dance is on the ninth, so we'll need to know within a couple of days. She'll need to buy the tickets from her camp leader, if you can go."

Seth's mind immediately filled with all kinds of reasons not to go. He was too tired from working so hard all the time to go dancing. He needed to catch up on work that had been piling up since he'd put in so many hours at

Gillian's place. He didn't want to become more attached to Gillian's sisters and feel yet another obligation.

But in the end, he looked into Kaylee's hopeful eyes and said, "What should I wear? Is it a tie thing, 'cause I don't own many ties."

Kaylee's little mouth spread into a giant grin. "See Mom? I told you he'd go." Then to Seth she said, "Yeah, I don't usually go 'cause I have to wear a dress, but Mom promised me a new one from over in Pigeon Forge. Maybe we can get you a tie if you need one."

No one, not even the most seasoned, calloused womanizer, could have refused her. The little tomboy had just offered to wear a dress and buy him a tie just so he'd escort her to a father-daughter dance. He wondered if she'd avoided the dance in years past due to the fact she hated dresses, or because she hadn't had a father to take her.

Well, he'd take her, and they'd show all the other little girls that Kaylee had someone in this town who cared about her, just like the other girls did. So what if he wasn't her dad? So what if he never wanted the responsibility of rearing children of his own? For one evening, they could both pretend.

He pulled some twenties from his wallet and handed them to Kaylee. "I'll tell you what, sport. You take that and go buy yourself a dress and shoes or whatever, and then you find me a tie that'll go with it. Your mom can help you." He winked at Patty and shook his head when she would have protested. "If there's anything left over, you guys can go on down to one of the amusement centers and take the go-carts for a spin. I hear there's a new elevated wooden track that'll knock your socks off."

The little girl's eyes lit up brighter than the fireworks from the night before, her expressiveness reminding him of Gillian at the same age. They were two peas in a pod.

"Thanks, Seth," she said, bills wadded up in her hand. "Do I have to share with Heather?"

He gently chucked her beneath the chin. "Yes, squirt, you do."

"Seth, that was too generous, but thank you," Patty said as soon as the girls said their good-byes and headed for the door. "It's a special night, and she's never been able to—"

"It's my pleasure, Patty. I'll be out to get her around six o'clock on the ninth, if that's okay with you."

Patty beamed. "That's just fine. See you then."

Seth watched as they all walked out together and half-heartedly muttered beneath his breath. How in the world had he gotten this mixed up with Gillian's family? All he needed was one more thing holding him back.

Gillian looked over at the adorable teddy bear she'd propped up on the settee and felt the most delicious tug at her heart. She'd slept with the thing last night, but it was a poor substitute for Seth. It was probably for the best that Seth had given her nothing more than a lingering kiss on her doorstep when he dropped her off last night, because she'd been so excited, so downright happy, that she might have actually gone and done the unthinkable. She might just have told Seth she loved him. Of course, by now, he probably had that figured out.

With a shake of her head, she mentally chastised herself for having gone and fallen for the guy. But it had been impossible not to. How could she resist a man who worked as hard as he did, who understood family responsibility as well as he did, though he'd deny it in a heartbeat. He was charming, sexy, and fun to be with, but Cupid's arrow had scored a direct hit when he'd rescued Kaylee from embarrassment by winning her the gigantic gorilla. Who could resist a man who cared so much about a little girl's feelings?

She dropped down on the settee and pulled the bear into her lap for a little cuddle while she contemplated her situation. So she loved Seth. What now?

She sighed. Nothing, that's what. It was something she'd

treasure forever like one of the trinkets she occasionally stumbled across in her acquisition of antiques. Birth certificates, baby pictures, letters—things forgotten by people who had once cherished them. She'd never forget, just as Maude hadn't forgotten her love for a man she could never have.

She'd known the letter was Maude's the moment Maude had recognized and identified the dresser as her own. At first, Gillian had thought Maude's angst had been over the dresser itself, but then she'd remembered the love letter, and it had all made sense. Maude had wanted the letter back. Of course, why she hadn't just come right out and asked for it, Gillian couldn't figure, but she imagined Maude had her reasons. She wondered what they were.

After reading it, she felt she understood Maude a little better. How sad it must have been to watch the man she loved marry another woman, knowing he was lost to her forever. She felt empathy for the older woman. The parallels in their situations weren't lost on her.

Gillian tucked the teddy bear back into place and pushed herself off the sofa. She was tired today from all of the excitement of her opening day and the festivities of last night, and she was suddenly feeling a bit melancholy. Thoughts of lost love tended to dampen one's spirit, and she wasn't in the mood to sit and feel sorry for herself. What she needed was a change of scenery.

After grabbing her purse and car keys from her office, she flipped the open sign that hung in the front window and turned the little clock hands to read: Will be back at twelve-thirty. Then, she climbed in her Rodeo and headed into town for lunch at the diner, harboring just the tiniest bit of hope she might run into Seth while she was there.

"Gillian!" Kaylee's excited cry could be heard clear across the crowded diner and couldn't have pleased Gillian more. She'd fallen head over heels in love with her sisters and was thrilled to know they felt the same. With a wave to let Kaylee know she saw her, she worked her way toward them.

"What are you guys doing out today? I thought you'd be home playing with all those stuffed animals Seth won for you last night. Either that or still sleeping," she said as she settled into the booth next to Kaylee.

Patty laughed. "They'd sleep until noon if I'd let them, but Kaylee made me promise to wake her up early today." She winked at her daughter and Gillian immediately knew something was up.

"Okay, spill it," she said, gently poking Kaylee with her elbow and earning a giggle. "What's so special about today?"

"Nothing." Kaylee squirmed and looked down at her lap, but not before Gillian caught the pink spots that appeared in the little girl's cheeks.

She looked at Heather and Patty questioningly, and Heather didn't disappoint her. "Kaylee's got a date with Seth for the Camp Girls' Father-Daughter dance. He gave her money to buy a dress and everything."

Gillian's heart fluttered as her eye flew to Patty's for confirmation. "Is that right?" Seth was going to be a stand-in father for Kaylee so she could attend a special dance? He'd given her money to go buy a dress, knowing the little tomboy wouldn't have one of her own to wear? *How sweet,* was her first thought; *Poor Kaylee,* was her next.

She took a closer look at her sister who now had her face buried in her arms. The girl was embarrassed to the roots of her hair, and Gillian knew why. He'd given a starving child the attention she so desperately craved, and now he was her hero. Kaylee was in love with Seth.

Oh, it was just puppy love, but a girl's first crush was nothing to dismiss lightly. Gillian knew that first-hand. Her first crush had been Seth too.

Did Seth realize what this would mean to Kaylee? To

step up and win her a stuffed animal at the carnival was one thing, but to stand in as a substitute father was another. If he planned to stick around for awhile and be a part of Kaylee's life, that was one thing, but he didn't. He was leaving, and at this rate, he'd be leaving a trail of broken hearts behind him. She was a big girl and could look after herself, but Kaylee was just a child. She'd already lost a father; could she handle losing Seth too?

Susie came over to take their orders, and by the time she left, Kaylee seemed to have recovered enough to munch on some fries. Gillian coaxed her into a conversation that was a little less threatening than speaking directly about Seth. "What kind of dress do you want?"

"Nothing too girlie," Kaylee said, screwing up her face. "Mom's taking us over to Pigeon Forge tomorrow to find one. They've got a bunch of stores over there, and Seth gave us extra money so we can go to the go-cart track, too. Wanna come?"

She'd have liked nothing better, but she had a store to run. "Maybe one Sunday when my store is closed we can all go together, but I've got to work tomorrow."

Kaylee accepted that with a nod and just a small sigh of disappointment. "If you made crafts like Mom you'd only have to work the weekends at the flea market," she advised, eliciting a moan from Patty and a laugh from Gillian. "Well, you could come to the dance then. The moms are serving punch and stuff. You could help."

The last thing she wanted to do was horn in on Kaylee's special night, but Patty jumped right on the idea.

"That's a great idea. You can help Heather and me at the refreshment table and then we'll all go out for dinner afterwards. It only lasts a couple of hours, so we won't keep you out too late. What do you say?"

Gillian turned to Kaylee and searched her eyes. "Are you sure?" At Kaylee's eager nod, she accepted. "Tell me when and where, and I'll be there."

Smiles broke out all around and, other than a small twinge of worry about Kaylee's tender feelings, Gillian felt happy to be included in her first real family event. It pinched her heart a little to know that Seth's role in their little family would be just for a night, when, in her mind, she could imagine something much more permanent.

Without a doubt, she knew this was exactly where she belonged. Sitting in a diner full of people she knew, having lunch with her family, discussing plans together. In a very short time, Ruby Valley had truly become her home.

Chapter Fourteen

She was beautiful. Her wild hair had been tamed into a becoming French braid that hung neatly down her back, her face scrubbed clean of its usual layer of dirt and grime. The tie she'd chosen for him, quite tasteful in hues of blue, perfectly matched the simple navy blue dress and shoes she'd chosen for the occasion. His heart constricted just looking at her. If he'd ever dreamed of having a daughter of his own, she'd have looked just like this. It struck him like a fist to the gut how much she favored Gillian.

He presented her with a delicate rosebud corsage, white with a ribbon of blue, then showed her how to fasten it with the band to her wrist. Then, after a few pictures for Patty's album, he escorted Kaylee to his truck, which he'd washed just for the occasion. Patty and Heather would follow later and meet them there, but the evening was for Kaylee and he planned on making her feel like Cinderella at the ball.

"What's on your mind, sport?" he asked, noting her uncharacteristic silence, hoping to ease her sudden bout of shyness.

She plucked at her dress and shrugged. "I look stupid in this dress."

Now Seth had dated enough women to know when one was fishing for a compliment, but this wasn't one of them, and it just about broke his heart. Her insecurities, hidden behind her tomboyish exterior, ran deep, reminding him of another little girl he used to know. Both had the same tough exterior protecting a soft core of feelings. You just had to know how to chip away at it until it cracked.

"Are you kidding me? You're going to knock the socks off of the other girls, just like when you hit the ball clear out of the ballpark and scored the winning run for your team last year at the state championship game. Remember how they put you up on their shoulders and carried you off the field?" Nearly the entire town had traveled over to Waynesville to watch that game, and her picture had made not only the local paper but the paper over in Charlotte as well.

She grinned. "Even Caroline Pinckney was nice to me that day, and she's never nice to anyone."

"Was that the whiny girl at the carnival?"

"Yeah. She's a real show off. Her dad owns the car place out on Highlands Road, and she's always getting new stuff all the time. She brags a lot."

Seth ran a hand over her braid and squeezed her shoulder gently. "Well, she didn't win a gorilla the size of a mountain, and she's not going to be any prettier than you are tonight, I can promise you that."

"You really think I look okay?" She wanted to believe him, he was sure.

"Better than okay, kid. You look awesome."

Her eyes sparkled and he could sense her relief. That hadn't been so hard. Maybe parenting wouldn't be the sheer torture he'd imagined. An image of a beautiful baby girl popped into his mind. She had strawberry curls and chubby little cheeks the color of Gillian's delicate skin beneath her sprinkle of freckles. He entertained the thought for about two seconds before he started to sweat and focused instead on the road ahead.

When they arrived at the community center, which had been transformed into a midnight garden complete with potted greenery and white twinkle lights suspended from the ceiling, Kaylee had another attack of shyness. She plastered herself to the far wall, as far away from the dance floor as possible. If the ficus tree had been a little bit fuller, she might even have taken refuge behind it. As it was, she was sitting as close to it as possible without climbing right into the black plastic pot. Sensing her anxiety, Seth didn't press her to move right away, but he soon realized she wasn't going to be pried away from the plant by anything short of an atomic bomb. Something had to be done, or the evening would be over before it had even begun.

Tomboy Gillian flashed into his mind. He could imagine her doing just this sort of thing when she was young. How many times had she run off to hide during her lifetime? Part of her must have wanted to attend a father-daughter dance with her dad, but she'd never have admitted it to anyone. He remembered when she'd been confirmed into the church at about this same age and had had to wear a white frilly dress. He'd told her she looked like a sissy and had earned a black eye for his trouble. By the time the church picnic was over, the dress had been muddied beyond recognition, earning Gillian a scolding from her mother.

He looked down at Kaylee and smiled. Perhaps he should try a different tactic than he'd tried with Gillian. What the little girl needed was a little loosening up.

"How do they move like that?" he asked, gesturing toward the dancers with his head while moving his shoulders and hips experimentally. "Am I doing it right?"

She looked instantly mortified. "Not like that!" she said, rolling her eyes and her shoulders at the same time. "You've gotta move your shoulders a little more."

"Like this?" He moved his shoulders, though in a more exaggerated fashion than she'd indicated.

She cringed. "That's not exactly right either. Watch me," she said, hopping up and moving in time with the beat.

Seth followed her lead until he managed to move to her approval, then he took her by the hand and led her out to the floor without a squeak of protest from her. He let out the breath he'd been holding and gave himself a mental pat on the back. His intuition had been right on target. She'd wanted to dance, but had been too shy. Every woman should be so easy to understand.

After dancing several songs in a row and finding ten new ways to make her laugh, Seth pleaded for mercy. "I'm old, Kaylee, I've got to take a break for a few minutes. Let's go get some punch and sit down for a little while."

"You go on," she said dismissively, no longer needing his protection, "I'll dance with my friends over there." He watched as she scurried over toward a group of girls who immediately gathered round, admiring her corsage. He scanned the room for her nemesis, Caroline, and smiled when he didn't see her anywhere. That was just as well in his book. He didn't want anything to mar the experience for Kaylee. Everything should be perfect for her tonight.

Satisfied she'd be just fine with her friends, he took her up on her offer of a reprieve, wondering when he'd gotten too old to dance. It was true he hadn't been out partying in over a year, but did a man loose his stamina that quickly?

Something cold was just what he needed at the moment, anything to cool him down a bit, but when he arrived at the refreshment table, he was surprised to find not just Patty and Heather, but Gillian as well.

"Gillian, ladies," he said, taking a punch cup from Gillian without touching her hand, deciding to play it as cool as possible for both their sakes. "What's up?"

"That's some funky dancing you've been doing out there," Heather said. "I'm glad I'm not a Camp Girl."

Seth held a hand to his heart as though she'd mortally wounded him. "What? Are you slamming my dancing abilities? Are you saying I wasn't movin' and groovin' better than any father out on that dance floor? You're crazy!" He looked from Heather to Patty, then to Gillian. "Help me out here, ladies. Tell this girl what talent I have. I'm a natural Fred Astaire."

Patty and Gillian groaned in unison and Heather asked, "Who's that? Isn't he some old guy actor or something? I saw him dance with a vacuum cleaner on a commercial, I think."

Now Seth was really wounded and soundly put in his place. "Have a heart, Heather."

Gillian came to his rescue. "I've danced with him Heather. He's really very good."

"And I'll prove it," he said, startling both of them by reaching out across the punch bowl and snatching her hand. "Dance with me."

She protested and pulled back, but he led her out to the floor anyway and swung her into his arms. The tune had changed, thankfully, from N'Sync to Travis Tritt, and he was relieved to be able to hold her again like he'd wanted to for the better part of a week now.

For a few moments, they did nothing more than sway together while Seth crooned softly with Travis, Gillian's forehead resting on his shoulder, but soon his mouth came perilously close to pressing a kiss to her temple. With regret, he pulled just far enough away so that he wasn't tempted. "How's it going with the shop?" he asked, searching for a safe topic of discussion.

"Fine so far, but I've only been open for a few days. It's a little too soon to tell."

He nodded and searched for something else to say. She was friendly enough tonight, but something about her smacked of coolness. "The Fourth was a success though, wasn't it?"

She nodded and answered politely, "Yes, it was very successful. Thank you for asking."

That was just a little too cool, and it was beginning to irritate him. "Let me take you home tonight." The words were out of his mouth before he knew he was going to say them, but he couldn't undo them and didn't really want to anyway.

"I don't need a ride, thank you. I'm riding with Patty and Heather to dinner, then they're taking me home. Besides, you're taking Kaylee home, remember? This is her night."

"I'll come back by after I drop her off," he said, his arms trying to urge her resisting body just a bit closer, wondering if he'd shock the whole town by kissing her right here on the dance floor.

She held firm. "Not a chance."

He searched her face, trying to read her expressive eyes, but the room was so dark he couldn't see her clearly, and it frustrated him. "What's going on, Gillian?" he asked.

The music ended and she stepped away, backing out of his reach. "Nothing, Seth. Just keep your mind on Kaylee. She's coming over." With that, she turned away and retreated behind the relative safety of the punch bowl, leaving him with his date for the evening.

"Let's dance," Kaylee said, and led him further onto the floor, closer to some of her friends, where she introduced him around.

Resigned to wait until later to settle things with Gillian, he glanced at her only once before firmly turning his attention back to Kaylee. It was her night, and he wanted it to be perfect for her so she'd have fond memories for years to come. Maybe she'd even have the confidence to come alone next year, or better yet, he could make plans to come back and take her if Charlie and the business could spare him for a weekend. If not, he'd talk Jackson into filling in, or maybe even Gillian could substitute for him. He ordered his wayward thoughts not to linger on Gillian, and tried to focus on the girls talking around him. He'd have plenty of time to ponder the subject of Gillian later on.

"I told you not to come." She was wearing a terry bathrobe that covered her from neck to mid-shin, yet he'd never thought her lovelier.

"I just want to talk to you. Come outside and sit with me awhile."

She hesitated for a moment, then came out onto the porch and shut the door behind her. "What?"

He took her arm and led her to the steps he'd yet to fix. They were probably in danger of falling through, but at least they wouldn't be in danger of letting passion muddy the waters of discussion.

"Sit down," he ordered, gesturing to the steps, a bit uneasy when she complied so easily. Settling down next to her, he got right to the point. "Why are you mad at me?"

Her silence lasted so long, he wasn't sure she was going to answer him, but finally she heaved a deep sigh and wrapped her arms protectively around her knees. "I'm not mad at you. It's not that easy," she said, burying her face in her bathrobe.

"Just tell me what's wrong, and I'll fix it." As with Kaylee earlier in the car, he felt her discomfort, but this time, he hadn't a clue what to do about it. He rubbed a hand across her shoulder, doing his best to comfort without understanding what was wrong.

She laughed bitterly and shrugged off his hand. "You think it's that simple? What are you going to do, Seth, take out a bottle of carpenter's glue and fix her heart when it's broken into tiny pieces?"

Now he was totally confused. "What in the world are you talking about?"

"Kaylee." She got up and paced the tiny porch, her soft, fuzzy slippers catching on the rotten wood with each step. "You've insinuated yourself into her life, taking on the role of father, and she's going to be hurt when you leave. I think you should stay away from her."

Seth was stunned. He'd thought he'd been doing a terrific job as a stand-in dad, giving an opportunity to Kaylee that she'd never before had. He'd felt great about doing it by night's end, and he knew Kaylee had been pleased. How could she find fault with that? "You're angry because I'm being nice to your sister? Well, someone has to be. She's a lonely little girl who doesn't get enough attention, so she hides behind her tough exterior so no one will know she's hurting. For some reason, she trusted me enough to ask the favor of escorting her to her dance. She opened up her shell just enough to let me inside, and I wasn't about to let her down." He stood up and halted Gillian's pacing, gripping her arm to hold her still, partly so she wouldn't walk away and partly so she wouldn't fall through the rotten boards. "She's just a scared little girl looking for a place to belong. Sound like anyone else you know?"

Bingo. He had hit the nail on the head. Her nostrils flared and her eyes lit with fire. He could feel her trembling beneath his hands and prepared for her attack.

"You're right, Seth. She is a scared little girl. She's afraid of being different from the rest. She's afraid of not belonging and being alone. Our father died before she even got a chance to know him, and she's afraid she's going to get left again one day. She's got feelings and they're so very fragile. Can't you see that? You have wonderful intentions, but you're going to hurt her if you let her get close to you." She yanked her arm free and ran down the steps to pace in the grass, putting distance between them when Seth wanted nothing more than to reach out and comfort her. "She's just a child, Seth, and she won't understand when you walk away. I think Maude's right about you. You complain about your family and their demands on your time, but I think you really like it when they all depend on you. I think it makes you feel important and powerful to know they're still going to need you when you walk away."

Anger gripped him so hard he went cold. "Maude said that?" he asked, forcing his voice through a throat suddenly too thick with emotion to speak. "She thinks I *want* all of them to depend on me and suck the life right out of me? If that's the case, then why am I walking away from it all?"

"If it's not the case, why have you waited this long to go? Why wait until September, Seth?" she questioned, temper, and something more, flashing in her eyes. "If we're such a strain on your precious time, why not leave now?"

Seth eyes narrowed dangerously, and he could have sworn his heart ground to a complete halt at that moment. "What did you say?"

"You heard me," she stated, standing now as still as a statue, tossing her challenge right in his face. "If you're going to walk out on your family, why don't you just go ahead and do it? What are you waiting for? What's keeping you here, Seth? Your cousins? Aunt Maude? Certainly not me. It couldn't be that you're afraid to find out we don't really need you after all, could it?"

"My cousins are my business partners, Gillian. I'm not walking out on them cold. I'm making sure they're able to run the store without my help before I leave. That's not fear; it's responsibility."

"That's so egotistical of you!" She balled her fists at her sides, and he was sure she'd be happy to use them on him, she was that riled up. "You've made sure they're all dependent on you for every little detail, seeing to their every need, running things the way you think they should be run, then when they can't make it without you, you leave them to fend for themselves. You *want* them to need you, Seth, but you don't want the responsibility of caring for them, so you're going to leave. That's *not* responsibility; that's running away!"

He laughed mirthlessly and felt his heart turn to ice.

"Look who's talking! Why are you here, Gillian? You think you came back to find something you lost, when it was right there with you in Florida the whole time. You may have lost your father, but you had your mother with you. You weren't alone in the world. You weren't running to something, Gillian, you were running away just like your mother did when she left your father."

Gillian reeled back as though she'd been slapped. She stood speechless as he walked down the steps past her to his truck. Remorse would probably sink in tomorrow, but tonight he wanted her to feel the same pain she'd made him feel. She'd wadded up his dream like so much trash and thrown it in his face.

Well, it was too bad if she didn't approve of his plans, because nothing and nobody would stop him from following them. Not Gillian, not his family, and certainly not a scrubby little tomboy who'd mistakenly thought he was her hero. He revved up his truck and peeled out of her drive onto Highway Twenty-eight, never once looking back in the rearview mirror.

Fiery red hair and a temper to match flashed into his mind, but he firmly blocked out the image. Before she'd come back to the valley, everything had been so much easier, so much clearer. No one had questioned him about leaving; they'd just waited for him to do it.

Well, maybe it was time he did. Tomorrow he'd give Charlie a call and let him know he was on his way. It was time to leave Ruby Valley, and all its encumbrances, behind for good.

Chapter Fifteen

The jangle of the brass bells suspended from the front door alerted Gillian to the arrival of her first customer of the day. Glad to have something other than Seth to occupy her thoughts, she put on a smile and walked out of her office to greet the newcomer. She drew up short at the sight of Elizabeth Connor. Had she come to get the juicy details of her fight with Seth?

"Good morning," she said, reluctant to talk about what had transpired between herself and Seth. She'd acted terribly and realized, after a sleepless night of self-reflection, she'd been more concerned about her own feelings of abandonment than anyone else.

"Morning," Elizabeth responded. "Wouldn't happen to have any coffee on, would you?"

"All day, every day," Gillian admitted. "I can't live without the stuff. Come on back." She turned and led the way to the kitchen where she grabbed a couple of jumbo mugs and filled them.

Elizabeth took her mug and settled in at the kitchen table. Gillian hesitated a moment, then followed her lead and joined her there, a bit apprehensive about what was to

157

come. For a few moments they sat quietly, until Gillian didn't think she could bear another moment of silence.

Elizabeth toyed with her coffee spoon, then pushed it aside. "Seth's gone."

Gillian's heart lurched, then plummeted to the bottom of her stomach. "When did he leave?"

"Yesterday. I thought Aunt Maude would've said something."

Gillian shook her head slowly and tried to get her heart beating again. "I haven't talked to her lately. Is he coming back?"

Liz nodded. "He's gone to find a place to live, but he'll be back for his things in a week or so. Charlie's probably doing a jig over there in Charlotte. He never really believed Seth would uproot and move, I don't think. The suddenness kind of took us all by surprise, I guess."

Gillian hung her head guiltily, replaying those horrible accusations in her mind. "I may have had something to do with that."

"I figured as much. Seth was on a tear the moment he walked through the door yesterday, barking orders at everyone in sight. You'd have thought he was a tyrant ruling his kingdom the way he had everyone scurrying to do his bidding."

"Yeah, that sounds like Seth, alright. So, if he was acting normal, how'd you figure I had something to do with it?"

Lizzie laughed. "Because the only time he's used my middle name in the past ten years was when he was ticked off about you. He's done it twice now. Besides." She shrugged. "He was even more obnoxious than ever. Whatever happened, it hit him hard. Thank goodness he was only around for a couple of hours before he left."

Gillian felt for Elizabeth. She'd seen the depth of his temper the night before. "Sorry."

Elizabeth shook it off. "Anything you want to talk about?"

Gillian recoiled from that. The words they'd exchanged were not for family ears. They would remain between Seth and Gillian if she had anything to do about it. There was no need to drag others in. "No thanks."

Elizabeth's dark eyes searched hers, as though trying to decide if she could drag the answers she sought from their depths, but in the end all she said was, "Well, if you want to talk sometime, give me a call. I promise to keep it between us."

Gillian believed her, but knew she would never tell her just the same. "I know you would," she said. "I trust you."

Elizabeth hugged Gillian, then left quickly, looking a little embarrassed by the uncharacteristic display of affection. Gillian was no less flustered. Who'd have thought she and Elizabeth Connor would ever become friends, and it would be Seth who brought them together?

The jingle of the doorbell called to her and she went out to find Aunt Maude standing in her parlor, an envelope in her hand. She wasn't sure she was ready to face another member of Seth's family just yet.

"I want you to have this." Maude said, thrusting the envelope into Gillian's hands. "It's the money Mr. Keeney gave me for the dresser."

Gillian looked inside and counted several hundred dollars, then tried to hand it back, but Maude wouldn't take it. "I can't take this, Aunt Maude. Especially after all the work you did around here to help me open up shop."

"Keep it," Maude urged her. "I wasn't here to help you out as much as I was here to search for my letter. I wasn't honest with you. Please keep it."

Knowing what it must have cost the woman to make such an admission, Gillian walked it to her cash box, unlocked it, and tucked the envelope inside, knowing she'd never keep the money for herself. Perhaps she'd donate it to the children's home or another worthy charity.

"Thank you," she said, wondering what had changed

Maude's mind about paying for it. "Would you like some coffee or tea?"

Maude shook her head and gestured toward the settee. "Would you sit for awhile? I have something to say."

Now Gillian was really uncomfortable. Was Maude upset by Seth's sudden departure? "Of course," she said and sat, pulling the teddy bear protectively into her lap.

"I owe you an apology, and it's not an easy one, so please just give me a moment to collect my thoughts."

Gillian searched Maude's face and could see whatever she'd come to apologize about was giving her troubles. She wished she knew how to put the other woman at ease, but she came up empty-handed, so she waited patiently, hugging the bear to her chest.

"I didn't offer my help getting your shop ready because I wanted to be nice or neighborly. I wanted my letter back, and I needed an excuse to look for it."

"Why didn't you just ask me about it?"

Maude sat down heavily next to Gillian. "I didn't want anyone to know about it, especially Seth. He was here working and I was afraid you'd come across it and show it to him. The chances of that were slim, but still, there was a chance."

Gillian thought about the contents of the letter and figured she could understand that. "I was discreet about it, but I don't see what difference it would have made to Seth. You're entitled to love, just like everyone else is."

Maude smiled sadly, "You were discreet, and I thank you. You returned it to me with no questions asked, but I have a question for you. Did you read it?"

Gillian flushed guiltily. "It fell out from behind a drawer while I was refinishing the dresser down in the basement. I read it and tucked it away into my box of treasures because I didn't think I'd find its owner. There were initials on it, but I don't think I ever would have linked it to you if you hadn't claimed the dresser. That's how I knew."

Maude looked pained for a moment. "It's a treasure to me too, but it's also a curse. It holds a secret that has the ability to ruin many lives, even though it happened so many years ago. I didn't want it to turn up in the wrong hands."

"You're lucky the Keeneys didn't get their hands on it. It was only signed with initials, but they'd have known it was yours the same way I did if they'd ever gotten around to restoring that dresser."

"They'd have known who it was intended for too, I'm afraid. I thought it would be safe hidden beneath the drawer that way. It's been there for nearly thirty years, you know."

"Well, I'm glad you have it back, and your secret's safe with me. What are you going to do with it now?"

Maude's look grew fierce. "I burned it." She stood up and walked to the window that overlooked her house. "I should never have written it in the first place, but I was young and in love. I made some bad choices, and I couldn't right the wrongs that I caused. Seth's mother suffered for my mistakes, but there's no reason for her children to suffer for them too." She turned back toward Gillian and looked her straight in the eye. "You need to make the right choices in this life, because it's the only life you're going to get. Making bad choices, selfish choices, will only hurt others for years to come." Her words were ominous, causing a chill to race up Gillian's spine.

"I'm not sure I understand," she said, wishing Maude would just come right out and say what was on her mind.

"Seth is gone."

Gillian closed her eyes and took a calming breath. "Yes, I heard."

"Then I'll ask you straight out." Maude walked back to face Gillian, who had risen from the settee. "Do you know what you're doing? Are you making the right choices?"

Making the right choices? What other choices did she have? She'd made the decision to move back to the valley. Seth was the one who'd chosen to move away. What was she supposed to do about it? What choices did she have here?

Maude walked to the front door and opened it. "I was in your shop the night of the storm. I used the key you gave me to let myself in. You nearly scared the life out of me when you knocked on my door that night. I'd just gotten back to the house and thought you must have seen me. I didn't want you to know."

Gillian nodded sadly. "I put that together the day you said the dresser was yours." At Maude's perplexed look, she explained, "You had a streak of mud on your face that night. I didn't think about it until later, but then I wondered. How would you have gotten muddy unless you'd been outside? What would you have been doing outside at midnight during a storm? It just didn't make sense until you claimed the dresser. Then I understood."

Maude asked with frightened eyes, "You won't tell anyone, will you?"

"No, Aunt Maude. Your secret's safe with me."

"You're a sweet girl, Gillian. Just don't be a stupid one like I was. Listen to your heart."

Listen to your heart. That would be a little easier if she knew what in the world her heart wanted.

Gillian sat at her little kitchen table, eating another frozen dinner and wondering what in the world she wanted. She had everything she'd ever hoped for right here in Ruby Valley. She had family, friends, a home. Her business was up and running, somewhat smoothly at that. She was proud of her accomplishments, thrilled with her life, and so lonely for Seth she could cry.

She'd run him off. Out of a misguided sense of protectiveness toward Kaylee, and her own hurt that she couldn't share her love with him, she'd pushed him away. She'd wanted to hurt him the way she was going to be hurt when he left. In the end, she was the one who was suffering. And Kaylee, who hadn't even had the chance to say goodbye.

She'd behaved badly, but she didn't know what to do to make it right. How could she mend fences with Seth and let him know she wished him only the best?

He'd be returning in a week or so, Elizabeth had said, to collect his things. Would he be willing to forgive her for her harsh words and let her make amends?

She frowned as she thought of Maude's words again. Maude had said that Seth's mother had suffered for her mistakes. Since Seth's father had been named John, it didn't take a detective to figure out that he'd been the object of Maude's love. No wonder she hadn't been pleased to know that Seth had sold her dresser with the letter still in it. That particular thirty-year-old secret still had the power to hurt people she loved. Well, her secret was safe with Gillian. She'd already caused enough hurt to last a lifetime. She wouldn't seek to cause any more.

If only she could turn back the hands of time and take the accusations back, then Seth could have followed his dream in his own time, without accusations or guilt dogging his steps. She thought of how her mother had nipped at her heels in the months just before her departure. Harsh words had been thrown at her, words of doom and gloom, prophesizing her failure. She'd carried them around like a weight until Seth and the others had shown her she really did belong here. She was ashamed to realize she'd done the same thing to Seth that her mother had done to her. Somehow, she had to make things right.

With determination, she jumped up from the table to grab the phone. She'd need Elizabeth's help. She might not be able to take back the words, but she could leave Seth with a better taste in his mouth than bitterness, and offer apologies so he could leave again without the burden of guilt. She might be broken-hearted, but she'd do it for him because she loved him, and he deserved to be happy.

After talking to Elizabeth, who promised to recruit some other family members, she felt a weight lift from her heart for the first time since she and Seth had argued. The words she'd thrown at him that night might as well have been weapons, and the damage they'd inflicted might not be easily repaired, but she had to at least try. With the help of her friends, she'd have one shot at making things right between them and giving Seth the guilt-free send-off he deserved.

She'd better make sure her aim was true.

Seth rubbed a hand around the back of his neck, trying to ease the tension that nearly six hours of driving had created, wishing he'd waited until tomorrow to come back to the valley. Putting it off till another day wasn't the answer, though. It was better to face the music and get this over with as quickly as possible.

It's going to be rough facing everyone, he decided as he pulled his truck into the cabin's drive. There were people he needed to see, things he needed to say before he'd be free to get on with things. His stomach clenched a little at the thought. Had he made the right decision?

He stomped up the steps to his cabin and let himself in the door, then shut it behind him, leaning heavily against it.

Follow your heart. Maude's words from the E-mail she'd sent him at Charlie's reverberated in his head like the peal of church bells after a wedding. Who would have thought inspiration would come from crabby old Aunt Maude? Maybe there was hope for the woman yet.

He pushed away from the door and walked to his bedroom to change. He'd promised Elizabeth and Jackson he'd meet them for dinner at six, and it was nearly that now. The three-hour drive from Charlotte took nearly twice that with the roads closed due to an accident or he would have already been out to see Gillian. He would cut the dinner short and go out to her place this evening. A few hours wouldn't make much of a difference now.

He grinned. Who'd have thought it? For the first time in eight years, he didn't feel rushed to leave. He had all the time in the world now, and instead of feeling stifled and imprisoned, he felt great, in spite of a stiff neck. In fact, he felt absolutely free. And it felt mighty good.

He pulled on a fresh shirt and buttoned it up, then slid into a fresh pair of blue jeans and boots. As an afterthought, he splashed on a little aftershave so he'd smell good for Gillian. He'd do just about anything if it would give him an edge.

Flaming red hair and soft green eyes came to mind, and he embraced the image. Soon, he'd be holding her close, and this time, he wasn't going to let her go. In fact, before any more hurtful words came out of either one of their mouths, he was going to kiss her senseless and make her forget what they'd said in the first place.

But it would have to wait until after dinner. He needed to clear some things up with his cousins right now. There were going to be some changes, and the sooner they got that settled, the better off they'd all be.

Liz, Jackson, and Suzie met him at the diner right on time at six. Only instead of going inside to eat, they told him they were going someplace new out Highway Twenty-eight, up toward Bryson City.

"I don't have time to go all the way out to Bryson City," he complained, but the three of them shanghaied him anyway, disregarding his protests, and he found himself captive in the backseat of Jackson's Camry with Elizabeth snickering next to him.

"Calm yourself, cousin, it won't take long at all," Liz said, reading him like a book. She knew he was anxious to get a move on so he could see Gillian.

Suzie and Jackson had taken the front, and if Seth didn't

know better, he'd think they were giving each other secret little glances. Lover's glances. That was an awful lot of progress on Jackson's part in just two weeks. A lot must have happened while he'd been gone.

That made him think of Gillian again. She was never far from his mind. In fact, halfway to Charlotte he'd nearly turned around and headed straight back to her. But he'd needed some time to think, to make sure he was making the right decision. And he'd needed to talk to Charlie, since it would ultimately have an effect on him.

He wondered if two weeks had changed her disposition any. The accusations she'd thrown around had had a lot of heat behind them. Could it be she wasn't just concerned for her little sister, but for herself as well? If he'd read her signals wrong, he'd just have to spend some extra time rewiring them, that's all. One way or another, Gillian was going to be his.

"We're here," Suzie announced, drawing Seth's attention from his thoughts and surprising him at the same time.

They couldn't possibly be anywhere close to Bryson City. They'd only been in the car for fifteen minutes or so. Curious, he looked out the window and saw Gillian's place just as Jackson slowed the car to turn in to the drive.

"What's going on, guys?" he asked suspiciously. Had they invited Gillian along for dinner, hoping to mend fences between them? Well, he could mend his own fences quite nicely and didn't really want to have an audience around while he was doing it. "Does Gillian know about this?"

"We're just stopping by for a minute," Liz explained, hopping from the car as soon as it came to a stop. She turned and called to Seth, "Come on, there's something you need to see."

The last thing Seth wanted to do now was see something in Gillian's shop, especially Gillian, but he figured since Jackson and Suzie had just abandoned him too, he might as well go along, if for no other reason than to hurry them up. He wanted to go get dinner over with, so he could come back and be alone with her. He desperately needed to talk to her as soon as possible. Resigned, he unfolded himself from the cramped backseat of the Camry and walked up to the shop.

"Surprise!" The entire shop sprang to life the moment he walked over the threshold. Everyone he knew, and then some, was there, surrounding him and pumping his hand, congratulating him on his move and new business.

Aunt Maude and Katie's crew were in the parlor, smiling from ear to ear at him. Jackson, Elizabeth, and Suzie were looking oh-so-proud of themselves for managing to get him to the shop without him being suspicious of their motives, and Patty and the girls were hovering around like busy little bees. Other faces were there, people he'd known all his life, but the person he most wanted to see was Gillian.

His eyes scanned the room, then found her observing quietly from her office doorway, looking totally isolated within the crowd. If he didn't know better, he'd think she was ready to bolt out of there and find a tree in which to hide. Wanting to make sure that didn't happen, he started to move toward her when Elizabeth grabbed him by the arm.

"Well, say something, dunderhead," she said, making everyone laugh and quiet down, putting Seth at a distinct disadvantage.

Totally taken aback, he couldn't manage to sputter anything more than, "Th-thank you, I guess." He wasn't going to tell her his news in front of the entire town. She needed to hear it first, then they could come back and make their announcements to everyone. If he had his way, the fact that he was staying put in Ruby Valley would pale in comparison to the other news he hoped to share. It had been awhile, but Ruby Valley was about to have itself another wedding, and soon.

Another round of laughter, accompanied by pats on the back, ensued as he lost sight of her. He disengaged himself as quickly as possible from the crowd and worked his way toward her now-empty office. "Where's Gillian?" he asked Patty as soon as he was able, fearing she'd bolted to parts unknown.

"Oh, she's hovering around here somewhere. Wasn't this nice of her to do for you? She wanted to make sure you got the send-off you deserve. She's so happy that you're finally following your dream of owning your own business and living in Charlotte."

Seth was a little taken aback by that. "She is? She said that?"

Patty smiled earnestly. "Oh yes. She's so happy here, and she wants for you to be happy too."

Seth's heart thumped a little harder in his chest. Had he read more into their relationship than existed? They were attracted to each other, but that didn't mean she wanted to marry him. Could he have been wrong about her feelings toward him?

He had to find her.

Aunt Maude got ahold of him first. "Did you get my E-mail?"

"Yes," he answered distractedly. All he wanted at the moment was to be left alone to find the woman he loved, and it seemed like an insurmountable task.

"Well? Did you take my advice?"

He looked at the woman who'd made the past few years of his life so very difficult, but he couldn't find it in his heart to tell her to mind her own business. For once in her life, she seemed to be trying to help. "Yes, Aunt Maude, I took your advice."

She smiled at him. "Good boy. Your parents would be proud of you. Now why don't you go find Gillian and tell her that; she's hiding out in the basement, I think."

He could have kissed her. Old Maude had come through

in a pinch. But what was Gillian doing down in the basement? Hiding out with the old, musty, forgotten pieces of junk she called antiques? He'd never figure her out, but he'd have a lot of fun trying, and he planned on having a lifetime to do it.

"Gillian?" he called into the dim basement, carefully descending the stairs. "You down here?"

A noise from behind an armoire drew his attention, and he watched silently as she emerged from its shadow. She was dressed in a soft pink sleeveless sweater and a pair of tan slacks, reminding him of the little pink tee she'd been wearing that first day he'd seen her all grown up. God, he loved her.

"What're you doing down here in the dark? You're missing the party." His hand itched to reach out and touch her, but it was still too soon. Once he started, he didn't plan on stopping anytime soon.

"It's your time. I just wanted to let you and your family and friends have a good time and say your good-byes." She kept herself at a safe distance, more than an arm's length away from him.

"It's not a party without you." He held out his hand for her, then dropped it when she didn't take it. "Come upstairs with me."

She shook her head, making her curls dance like angels around her face. "I think I'll just say my good-byes right here, if you don't mind. I've never been very good at them."

"Look, if you're still mad at me, I'd like a chance to explain myself, but," he looked around at the dark, dusty basement, lit only by her work light, "not here." When he told her of his plans, he wanted the setting to be perfect.

"It's not that," she said, looking at her feet, then at the rafters above his head. Anywhere but directly at him, he noticed. "I know I provoked you. I hope you've been able to forgive me for what I said."

"Gillian—" he started, but she quickly interrupted him.

"No, Seth, let me finish. I want to thank you for all the things you did for me when I came back to Ruby Valley. You fixed up my shop so beautifully and only charged me a fraction of what the work was worth, I'm sure. You helped me meet wonderful people, including my lovely little sisters, and you were a good friend. You helped me realize my dreams, and now I'm helping you realize yours. I'm just returning the favor."

"Listen, Gillian, there's something I need to tell you—" he tried again, but again she cut him off.

"My parents' marriage convinced me that it's not for me. When I imagined myself here, I never envisioned sharing it with . . . well, you. Or anyone, for that matter. It was nice spending time with you, but my business is my life. I realize I may have given you a different impression the other night, and I wanted to clear it up before you leave again." She laughed, a brittle little laugh that made him want to shake her. "Believe me, my heart belongs to this shop and it will go on beating after you've gone."

Seth was flattened. He felt like he'd been run over by a steamroller, and it would take a putty knife to pry him up off the floor. He'd been wrong about her feelings for him. Totally wrong.

He looked at her hard, trying to see what was in her mind, her heart. But all he could see were shadows cast upon cool, moss-green eyes, telling him she spoke the truth.

Follow your heart. Maude's words came back to taunt him. Follow your heart until it led you to heartbreak? What kind of advice was that? He'd have been safer to have stayed in Charlotte with Charlie than to have sold out his share of the business and returned home to her. Now, he'd have to either get a new dream, or stay in Ruby Valley and live near her, remembering each time he saw her that he'd been cuckolded by love.

"I've given up on dreams, Gillian. They're not all they're

cracked up to be. Nothing but head games we play with ourselves." He stepped forward and put a finger to her lips to shush her when she tried to speak, touching her for the last time. "The problem with dreams, Gillian, is they go away when you wake up and then you find yourself alone with reality."

She shook her head and backed up a step to have her say, "That's not true, Seth," she insisted, with just a hint of fire beneath her cool exterior. "Don't give up on your dreams. Mine came true, didn't they?"

His chest was so tight, he wasn't sure he could breathe, but he managed to drive one last point home. "Did they, Gillian? Is this all you ever wanted and all you'll ever need? Well, I hope your dreams keep you warm at night. North Carolina winters can get pretty cold."

Her heart was breaking. She'd never felt so cold, so alone in her life. Seth's words had sliced right through her like a sword of ice, cutting away the lies, exposing ice-cold truth. All of her winters would be cold. Her dreams were nothing without him.

She could never tell him that, though. He could never know she loved him more than any dream she'd ever had for herself, because she never wanted to hold him back from achieving all he wanted in life. He wanted freedom. She could give him that, even if it meant denying her love for him. In her heart, she only wanted him to be happy.

She'd locked up the shop for the night after everyone left and was now lying alone but for the teddy bear in her bed. *Where is he now?* she wondered. How long would he be in town before he left for good? Not long, she hoped. She didn't think she could take it if he was around much longer.

Maude's letter came to her mind, and she wished she could read it again. She remembered reading it and wondering how a person could have been so selfless as to watch the man she loved marry another. Now she knew. Charlotte might not be a woman, flesh and blood, but she was very much the mistress of his heart. He'd lived and breathed for her for nearly a decade, and Gillian was willing to stand aside so he could have her.

He'd said that dreams went away when you woke up, but that was just because he'd never gotten to live his. Not yet, anyway, but soon he would. Then he'd know how perfectly they could turn out. Like hers had, with the exception of losing Seth when she'd just found him again. Of course, he'd never been part of the original dream, but how could he have been? She hadn't known she'd fall in love with him. He was an addendum to her dream. People had a right to change their minds about things, didn't they?

She flopped back on the bed and stared at the moonbeams streaming through her window. No one had ever warned her that love, true love, hurt like this. Thank goodness she'd never have to endure something like this again, because she was as sure as the night was dark that she'd never again love anyone like she loved Seth Connor.

Chapter Sixteen

Seth's mood was darker than a moonless night, and he wasn't hesitating to take it out on just about anyone who dared cross his path. For the past week, since his going-away party, most everyone had been wise enough to stay clear of him, with the notable exception of Elizabeth, who'd never had a lick of sense when it came to avoiding trouble.

"What's eating you?" she finally demanded, hands on hips in battle stance. "I can't take it anymore, so spill it or get over it. It's not even eight A.M. yet and already you've bitten my head off twice! Don't you have someplace to go—like back to Charlotte?"

Seth scowled at her and barked, "Can it, Liz. I don't need your advice. If you don't like my attitude, then go home or something. Stay out of the way."

Her jaw dropped. "If I didn't care about you so much, I would, but I do, so I can't." His scowl did nothing to deter her from her mission of helping him. "Look, Seth. Talk to me here. It doesn't have to be about what's bothering you. Let's talk about business."

He tightened his jaw, his impatience growing. "I'm not up for a chat just now, Mary Elizabeth. I'll let you know when I'm ready." He brushed past her, leaving her standing alone on aisle four.

"Oh," she said, running after him. "It's Gillian, isn't it? You used my full name, and you only do that when you're upset about her. What's she done now? Refused to go out with you? Refused to return your phone calls?"

That did it. Seth came to a complete halt, causing Liz to practically run him over when she didn't stop in time. Turning around, he caught her by the shoulders and set her back on her heels. "She refused to marry me."

Elizabeth was stunned. He could see it in her face, and he would have laughed if the circumstances were any different, but they weren't. And he wasn't laughing.

"I didn't know you'd asked her," she said, obviously at a loss. "But, Seth, you knew she wouldn't leave and go to Charlotte with you. I mean, she just got here and bought Bachelor's End and all. You didn't expect her to just pick up and follow you, did you?"

Now that he'd told her, he felt deflated. For the past week he'd run full speed on sheer anger, but he couldn't keep up the pace any longer. No matter how hard he worked, he couldn't outrun the hurt Gillian had caused him. There was a gaping hole where his heart had been, and nothing with which to fill.

He put his arm around his cousin and quietly walked her into the office where they'd have a bit of privacy. He needed to talk about it.

"I sold out to Charlie, Liz. I'm not going to Charlotte."

Her eyes nearly bulged right out of their sockets. "What? You can't possibly mean that. You've been wanting out of Ruby Valley for as long as I can remember, and you just blew your only chance? What's wrong with you?"

Seth shook his head ruefully. "You just said it, Liz. I've been wanting out of Ruby Valley." He ran a hand through his hair, trying to clear his jumbled thoughts. "I wasn't so much running *to* something as I was running away. I wanted away from responsibility. I guess that's what our family has always meant to me. I took on responsibility when our dads died and never let go. Then, I blamed you all for expecting me to do it."

"Seth, I'm so sorry." Liz reached out and laid a comforting hand on his shoulder. "You always took control and made it look so easy. We let you because you're really good at it. You know we can all stand on our own two feet around here."

Seth hugged her tightly. "I know, Lizzie. That's why I'm going to go into business for myself, but not in Charlotte. I'm opening my own construction company right here in Ruby Valley."

"Why didn't you say so? That's wonderful!" She planted a noisy kiss on his cheek, then backed up a step and cocked her head. "So then, what's the problem with Gillian? You told her you're staying, and she still turned you down? That just doesn't make sense. It's obvious she's crazy about you."

"Obvious to everyone but her. She threw me that going-away party and sent me packing. She said she doesn't want to share her life with anyone else. I wasn't part of her dream."

Liz laughed. "Seth, something's not adding up here. Give me some help with this. You told her you're staying, and she said she doesn't want you to?"

Seth hung his head and scratched at the whiskers he hadn't bothered to shave off that morning. "I didn't tell her I'm staying, but she made it clear she doesn't want anything to do with me."

Elizabeth smacked her forehead. "You dolt! Don't you see? She doesn't want you to stay here out of love for her and deny yourself your own dreams. She pushed you out of the nest so you could fly." When he didn't say anything she added, "When she heard you'd gone she called me to help her arrange the little surprise party. She said you'd had a terrible fight and she wanted to make amends before you left for good."

Seth knew that much. "So?"

"So, she wanted you to think she was happy for you. She doesn't want to be a ball and chain."

Hope came alive in his heart like the first delicate embers of fire. Could Liz be right? Could Gillian have sent him packing out of love?

Elizabeth fanned the flames. "If she doesn't want to share her business with anyone, why did she just convince Patricia to join her? They're turning the upstairs into a craft shop and calling it Patty's Attic," Elizabeth said, fanning the fire just enough to make it catch. "And what about her little sisters? She's sharing a life with them, too. It's not like she's a recluse, you know." Fan, fan.

The fire took hold and flamed up inside him. How could he have believed her when she said she didn't love him? She'd hidden out in the basement the night of the party rather than joining the rest in wishing him well. She'd been hiding her feelings from him. What an idiot he'd been to believe her.

With a kiss of thankfulness planted on Liz's cheek, he ran from the store and brought his truck to life, revving the engine and peeling out of the parking lot and around to the loading dock. There, he enlisted Jackson's help, rapidly issuing orders, and soon had his truck loaded with everything he needed to make his point to one stubborn, and rather misguided, redhead.

Heart brimming with determination, he headed out onto the highway toward Bachelor's End. He had a woman to set straight and a new life to begin, and he didn't want to waste a single moment more than he already had.

The droning whine of a power saw jolted Gillian out of the only sleep she'd managed to pull off in a week. With a groan, she pulled her pillow over her head and burrowed under, hoping to salvage just a bit of the sweet oblivion she'd so briefly found. At least until sanity set in and she realized there was no reason for anyone to be running a saw outside her cottage.

"What in the world," she muttered, dragging herself out of bed, stumbling over the tangled sheets that had looped around her ankle like clinging kudzu vines. Her head reeled from rising too fast and she nearly tumbled backwards onto the bed again. With a groan she kicked free of the sheet and, bent on doing somebody bodily harm, headed for the front door.

"What do you think you're doing!" she shouted as she opened the door, irritation propelling her forward across her rickety porch before she realized the steps were no longer there. With her heart in her throat, making a scream impossible, she launched off the edge and was caught hard against Seth's body, his capable arms holding her fast.

"Slow down there, Sparky," he admonished. "You almost took a header."

The adrenaline rush, or perhaps being held so closely against Seth, had her trembling in his arms. She pushed to free herself, wondering if her legs would hold her up when they finally reached the ground again. "Put me down!" she ordered, and he did, letting her slide intimately down the length of his body, reminding her she was rather skimpily dressed in her pink tee and gym shorts—again. With an unladylike snort, she backed up as far as the porch edge would allow and crossed her arms over her stomach.

"What are you doing here?" she demanded, totally confused, totally frustrated by his presence. He'd haunted her every thought for the past week, torturing her with dreams of what might have been, and now he was here in the flesh. Why couldn't he just have mercy and go away like he was supposed to? She'd nobly given him the freedom he wanted without standing in his way, and here he was standing smack-dab in the middle of hers.

Then he grinned that lopsided, little-boy grin and very nearly sent her right over the edge of what remained of her sanity after a week of longing for him. "What am I doing *here*," he asked, gesturing toward the sawhorse, "or what am I doing here, in general?"

"Here! Both!" She stamped her foot in exasperation. "Seth, why aren't you gone yet?"

His dark eyes danced merrily behind his safety goggles as his grin widened, and she bristled. She'd never liked being the object of someone else's amusement, especially Seth's, and it was obvious he was enjoying this moment. "I'm fixing your porch."

It was all she could do to keep herself from growling at him. "Why aren't you gone yet?" she repeated.

"Unfinished business," he said, as though that should explain it all. Then he turned back to his work, picking up a long board and positioning it against the saw blade. He flipped a switch and pushed the lumber through the grinding teeth, cleanly cutting one end off the length. When he reached for another, she thought she'd clock him with a two-by-four.

Unfinished business? What kind of explanation was that? "Wait!" she shouted before he could get started again. "Just wait right there, Seth. I don't want you doing this."

He looked behind her at the missing steps. "I think I'd better go ahead and finish or you're going to have a heck of a time climbing up to the porch."

He had her there. "Well, I told you I couldn't afford this right now, so you're working for free, you know."

"We agreed on payment, Gillian," he reminded her with a wink. "You owe me dinner, remember?"

She couldn't believe it. Seth was being as charming as ever, acting like nothing out of the ordinary was going on, while she was dying inside all over again. After her great display of acting like she didn't love him, that she wanted him to get on with his life, she'd taken pains to avoid going anywhere he might be. For two weeks she'd been practically a recluse, seeing only Patty and the girls and customers, just to make sure they didn't cross paths before he left town for good, and now he was her on her doorstep, so to speak, expecting her to cook dinner for him?

"I don't cook," she said, as soon as the saw was quiet again.

"I'm a decent cook when I put my mind to it. I'll teach you," he offered, turning back to her. He pulled off his safety goggles, tossing them on the grass near the sawhorse, and wiped the sawdust off his hands and clothes. She wanted to run her hands through his hair to free the tiny pieces of dust collected there, so she curled her hands into fists and tucked them tightly beneath her arms.

"No thanks. I'll give you a gift certificate to McDonald's," she said, warily watching him as he slowly moved closer.

"Eating out's going to get old pretty quickly. Besides, with both of our businesses just getting off the ground, I don't think we'll be able to afford it. Cooking at home's more cost-effective."

She turned and took a giant step up onto the porch to put some distance between them. It gave her a decided height advantage, which she enjoyed for about five seconds before he climbed up too. Her blood began to pump thickly through her veins as he continued his steady approach.

"We'll start with something simple like spaghetti," he said, gently fingering the thin strap on her shoulder once he had her backed up against the front door. Her heart picked up its pace, and her breath came a little faster. "You know how to make a salad, don't you?" The back of his finger grazed the delicate skin over her collarbone, and she thought she'd melt right at his feet.

Her eyes shut tightly as she tried to gather her topsy-turvy emotions. If he continued this, she'd be in his arms in another moment, and then he'd know the truth. She didn't ever want to let him go. Throwing pride out the window, she pleaded, "Please go, Seth. This is too hard." A single tear escaped and rolled unchecked down her cheek as her heart broke into a thousand tiny pieces.

His lips caught the tiny droplet at the corner of her mouth, just before he crushed her to him. "Gillian, I can't go, sweetheart. I'm not going anywhere," he said, as he rained kisses across her face, then buried his face in her hair.

Her heart took flight, then plunged just as swiftly back to earth. "But your dreams," she reasoned. "It's what you've always wanted. You can't stay here any more than I can go with you."

His quiet laughter wasn't what she expected, nor were the words that followed. "Living without you isn't a dream; it's my worst nightmare. Dreams change, people change." He threaded his fingers through her hair and pulled her back far enough to look her in the eye. "I've changed, Gillian. I love you."

Hope rose again in her heart like the sun over the mountains. Could love really be enough to hold him here with her, without regrets of dreams not followed? "But your family . . ."

"Will probably drive us both insane, but that's what families do. We'll just have to add to our own little family so we can eventually outnumber them." His lips grazed hers again while her senses spun out of control. "In fact, if you don't go put on something other than this little pink number, we'll be starting that family before you know it." He nuzzled her neck and growled, rubbing his whiskers against her tender skin, earning a little snort of laughter for his troubles. "I love it when you do that."

She captured his face in her hands and pulled him in for a long, heady kiss, leaving them both shaking when it was over. "And I love it when you do that," she said, pulling his head down for another.

"Gillian, you accused me of running away, and you were right. I knew it all along in my heart, but I'd never admitted it to myself. I try to be honest with myself, but that one I messed up on. Thank God you came along to set me straight before I made the biggest mistake of life." He framed her face in his trembling hands, his eyes delving deeply into hers, willing her to believe the truth of his words. "You've been in my heart forever, and my life will never be complete without you. Make my dreams come true and marry me."

She wanted to trust him. "How do I know you won't change your mind in five or ten years and regret staying here? What then?"

He kissed her tenderly on her cheek, then found her lips and kissed her again. "There aren't any guarantees in life, Gillian, but there are regrets by the million. All I know is if I walk away from you and Ruby Valley, I'll regret it for the rest of my life."

"My mother hates you, you know," she said. It sounded ridiculous, but she wanted him to know exactly what he was getting himself into before it was too late. "Eventually, she'll work her way up here, just to see if I've failed at making a go at the shop. And, of course, we'll have to invite her to the wedding."

Seth chuckled between dropping kisses onto her face. "We'll sic Aunt Maude on her if she causes any trouble. She's on our side."

Gillian nodded mindlessly. Seth's kisses were doing delicious things to her insides. "I know. She told me to follow my heart, but I thought that meant I had to let you go."

"She told me the same thing, sweetheart, but I knew it meant that I couldn't let you go. You need to learn to trust me a little. I'm usually right."

Gillian could argue the point if she put her mind to it, but at the moment her mind was too preoccupied with the kisses he was trailing up and down her neck.

"Gillian, I'm dying here," he whispered in her ear, even as he kissed her there. "Make my dreams come true. Will you marry me?"

As luck would have it, dreams were her specialty. "Far be it from me to deny a dying man his dreams."

And without so much as a touch of carpenter's glue, he took the tiny slivers of her broken heart and healed it with his love, making all their dreams that really mattered come true.